"Hi ...

"My na...

"Callie," the gir... ...smile as she pushed herself off from the ground a bit to start the swing going again.

Buffy cursed herself for not having paid more attention to Giles, but thought that the name did sound vaguely familiar. Hopeful that she was on the right track, Buffy rose and took the swing next to Callie's before she continued.

"It's kind of late . . . or kind of early, to be playing, isn't it?" Buffy asked. "Do your parents know you're here?"

The girl shrugged and continued to swing.

"You know, the swings were always my favorite too. But I hate to think that someone might be out there missing you right now. Why don't you let me walk you home?" Buffy suggested.

"I'm hungry," was Callie's defiant response.

"Okay," Buffy said, rising and extending her hand to Callie. "Come to think of it, I'm pretty hungry too. Maybe we could find a little something on the way back to your house."

"Do you like to eat people?" Callie asked sweetly. "Because I don't."

Buffy the Vampire Slayer™

One Thing
or Your Mother

Kirsten Beyer

**An original novel based on the hit television series
created by Joss Whedon**

SIMON SPOTLIGHT ENTERTAINMENT
New York   London   Toronto   Sydney

S|S|E

SIMON SPOTLIGHT ENTERTAINMENT
An imprint of Simon & Schuster Children's Publishing Division
1230 Avenue of the Americas, New York, New York 10020
™ & © 2008 Twentieth Century Fox Film Corporation. All Rights Reserved.
All rights reserved, including the right of reproduction in whole or in part in any form.
SIMON SPOTLIGHT ENTERTAINMENT and related logo are trademarks of Simon & Schuster, Inc.
Manufactured in the United States of America
First Edition 10 9 8 7 6 5 4 3 2 1
Library of Congress Control Number 2007928096
ISBN-13: 978-1-4169-3632-9
ISBN-10: 1-4169-3632-7

*For Patricia A. Beyer
and her mother,
Jewell Pellegrino*

My Watchers

ACKNOWLEDGMENTS

Patricia and Fred. Their sons, Matthew and Paul. Matthew's wife, Beth. Vivian. Her mother, Ollie. Her daughters, Debra and Donna. Their spouses and children, Bill, Michael, Justin, Chris, and Derek. Madeline and Bob. Their daughters, Elizabeth and Katherine. Anna. Heather. Samantha. Her husband, Sean. Their children, and my godchildren, Katey, Maggie, and Jack. Allan and Candy. Their daughters Christiana and Carolina. Fred and Marianne. Their son, Freddie. Tony. Vanessa. Cappiello. Tara. Art. Brett and Jenn. Jolene. John. Maura. Patrick. Emily. Cara.

To you, these names may not mean anything. To me, they mean the whole world. They are my family, my friends, the people who made me who I am, and who, one way or another, made this project possible.

Special thanks to Katherine for the title. To Heather, for the always helping me find my way when I'm lost. To Emily, for the opportunity. To Cara, for her careful editing. And to my mother, Patricia, and my grandmother, Jewell, for being nothing at all like the villain of this piece. I, too, know how lucky I am.

Joss Whedon is a genius. His work inspired mine, long before I had the chance to write about Buffy Summers. I am also indebted to the writers of *Buffy the Vampire Slayer*, and to the actors who brought their characters to such dazzling life.

Finally, David. He teaches me daily that there is nothing love cannot accomplish. Whatever I am, whatever I might achieve, it means nothing without his constant patience, understanding, support, and selfless devotion.

Thanks, guys.

Chapter One

Three to one wouldn't normally be considered the best odds to take in a fight. Of course, the math changed a bit if the "one" in question happened to be Buffy Summers. Technically, she was a vampire slayer. But the fine print of her unwritten contract with the powers that be didn't distinguish between vampires, demons, witches, ghosts, or any other purveyor of paranormal power that happened to make its way to Sunnydale, California, Buffy's home, and one of only a few cities on the planet whose claim to fame was being situated on a Hellmouth. Sunnydale's tourist brochures would never highlight this particular piece of trivia, because Buffy and a few of her closest friends were among the handful of folks who even knew what a Hellmouth was, let alone that its proximity to the quaint Southern

California town made it a magnet for all things evil.

"Tell me the truth," Buffy said as she landed a solid kick to the chest of one of her assailants that sent him crashing into a really lovely marble headstone. "You got that jacket at David Lee Roth's yard sale, didn't you?"

The vampire on the receiving end of her barb was too busy trying to pull himself up to find a witty retort. Buffy briefly considered pulling her favorite stake out of her jacket pocket and finishing him right then and there with a quick lunge and thrust. Unfortunately his buddies, whom she had already dubbed Tweedle-Dumb and Tweedle-Dumber, were regrouping to lurch at her from opposite flanks. Not to mention the fact that part of her, a tiny, secret part that she rarely gave this much rein, was thoroughly enjoying pounding these three losers to a pulp. The adrenaline coursing through her veins—and pushing her enhanced strength and fighting skills to their limits—had already worked her up into a satisfying righteous rage. Though the three punching bags she was currently working weren't really the source of her anger, she decided that for now she could settle for making them suffer a little for Angel's betrayal and his perverse sense of revenge before sending them off to their dusty and final oblivion.

"Come on, guys," Buffy taunted, backing up a little to keep Dumb and Dumber in her peripheral sightlines. "I get that you're new to this whole 'creature of the night' gig, but I know you can do better than this."

Dumb decided to feint to his right, a move he

telegraphed as clearly as if he'd written Buffy a memo beforehand, complete with a color-coded diagram of their fight. As she shifted her weight to counter, Dumber charged Buffy's back, throwing his whole weight into his attempt to knock her to the ground before baring his fangs and going in for a good long gulp of Slayer blood.

That was certainly the plan, anyway.

Unfortunately for Dumber, it took more than what had probably been in life the frame of a slight accountant to knock Buffy off her feet. Instead, she took his weight and used his own momentum to send him flipping over her back, feetfirst, into Dumb, who had unintentionally lined himself up perfectly to receive the full force of his accomplice's misguided efforts. Had this particular move been attempted by the Van Halen wannabe, it might have been a different story. He had a good fifty pounds on his buddies, and as strong as Buffy was, her petite frame was hardly invincible. Lucky for Buffy, strength wasn't everything in these nightly death matches. Speed and skill counted for much more than brute force, as she had learned again and again in the years that she'd been slaying vampires.

As Dumb and Dumber were busy untangling themselves from each other, poor David Lee Wrong had finally come to his senses and regained his feet. Instead of jumping back into the fight, he seemed to be seriously considering the better part of valor, also known as making a run for it.

Oh no, you don't, Buffy thought as he turned to

find his escape route. Without pause, Buffy grabbed her trusty stake and sent it flying through the air, straight through his back and into his heart. Though she couldn't see the expression on his face, she did hear a faint "Bummer, dude," as what had begun as dust quickly turned once again to dust, exploding into a million tiny fragments with a satisfying *whoosh*.

Unfortunately, the sense of minute accomplishment that usually followed the death of a vampire did nothing to assuage Buffy's anger. She turned back to the idiot twins who remained, fully prepared to finish the fight, hoping against hope that in the process some of the feelings she'd been struggling to wrestle into submission would find release.

For the moment, both Dumb and Dumber were staring in disbelief at the untimely defeat of their compatriot.

"Sorry, guys," Buffy said in the world-weary tone she often adopted when confronting newly risen vampires. "I know you haven't had time to read the handbook or attend any of the meetings, but here's how this works. Whoever makes the rules decided a long time ago that if vampires like you were going to treat this planet like an all-you-can-eat buffet, there would be at least one girl in every generation—that would be me—born with the strength and skill to balance the scales a little bit." Taking the bull by the horns, Buffy rushed the two vampires and, grabbing Dumber firmly by the lapels of his rayon-blend suit jacket, lifted him off his feet and tossed him atop Dumb before continuing.

"So, much as I regret raining on your parade," she

said, punctuating her remarks with a swift kick to Dumber's side which sent him rolling off Dumb, "it's my sacred duty to see to it that stupid"—another kick—"ugly"—a good stomp—"bloodsucking losers like you"—a final kick to Dumber's backside—"never have a chance to hide from the light of day."

Neither of her remaining foes was putting up much pretense of a fight any longer, and though Buffy hated to see this come to an end, she knew it was long past time. Grasping an overhanging branch, she pulled it from its resident tree and snapped it in half. With less ceremony than she would have liked, she thrust the first half through Dumber's back. As he exploded into dust, she turned on Dumb, who had risen to his knees.

"That sucks," he said weakly, already sensing the inevitable.

"Tell me about it," Buffy replied, finishing him off with the second half of the branch.

Buffy's rage ebbed ever so slightly as she placed her hands on her knees and caught her breath in the lonely cemetery.

It did suck.

It sucked more and harder than anyone in the world could possibly imagine.

The battle had been good. But that was little comfort. The battle she needed to fight right now was with her former boyfriend, Angel, the man who had taught her both the meaning of love, and the definition of tragedy.

She should have known it would never work. Truth be told, she had known. He was a vampire, and she was a Slayer. It was classic "Do not enter" territory.

Angel.

A vampire, yes. But not just any vampire. As foul and demented a demon as had ever walked the earth, he had once delighted in the infliction of exquisite pain on anyone unfortunate enough to cross his path. It was ultimately a camp of gypsies who had found a way to make him pay by giving him back the one thing that could make him truly regret his violent ways: his soul. By the time he had first met Buffy he'd had over a hundred years to wrestle with that soul and come to terms with the only choices before him. He could remain in the shadows of the world eking out a meager existence, or he could re-enter the fight on the side of the good and somehow try to redeem himself. He had made the harder choice. But with Buffy by his side, redemption had slowly begun to seem possible. Long before they had admitted their love to each other, he had proved time and again that he would always be there for her, protecting the Slayer when he needed to, supporting her whenever he could, and always fighting beside her through the worst the world could throw at her.

So in what universe was it fair that actually loving Buffy was the thing that destroyed him? The curse that restored his soul came with a little known caveat: If he ever knew real happiness, the soul that was meant to torment him would be taken from him. He had known happiness, and Buffy had known it with him, ever so briefly. And now Angel was gone. Worse than dead. A demon now wore his face, and since his transformation a few weeks ago he had done everything in his power to taunt, terrify, and torture the girl who had risked everything to love him.

It was like a bad dream that just wasn't ending.

Every time Angel had confronted Buffy since that fateful night when her world had changed forever, she had come closer to accepting the unacceptable. Angel was dead, and she was going to have to find it within herself to kill the monster that now roamed Sunnydale in his guise. And she had almost reconciled herself to that fact. Until a few days ago, when two frustrated ghosts, James and Grace, who had shared their own star-crossed affair over fifty years ago, had possessed Buffy and Angel in an attempt to resolve their issues.

Buffy could have done without the bad drama that was their last moments on earth. But she couldn't deny, even now, the unutterable joy that had washed through her when Angel had pulled her into his arms, talking only of love and forgiveness, and sealed that bond with the deepest and most passionate kiss they had ever shared. How much of what she had felt had truly belonged to James and Grace, Buffy would never know. What she did know was that feeling Angel's love again, even briefly, had made it harder than ever to accept the fact that what she'd once had was now gone forever, and for her and Angel there would be no fairy-tale reconciliation.

Taking a quick scan of the rest of the cemetery, Buffy decided that she'd probably seen all the action this particular location had to offer for the evening. She still had hours of homework waiting for her before she was going to be able to get some sleep. Finals were only a few weeks away and despite her best efforts, her classroom performance had been seriously subpar this semester. With a sigh, Buffy turned away from the neat rows of headstones and trudged toward the cemetery exit.

She had to admit that the last few nights her patrols had been particularly fruitful. She'd bagged more than a dozen newly risen vampires. In the days past, this would have been cause for pride, if not a small celebration. Now, the victory seemed strangely hollow. Buffy had decided a long time ago that there needed to be something, not much, but a little something more to her life than being the Slayer. She wanted a place she could call her own, a tiny garden inside of her that she could quietly tend and fiercely protect from the rest of her life. She'd found that and more in loving Angel. But now, Angelus had made it perfectly clear that he was taking special care in his plans to crush the heart and spirit of the Slayer before he took her life. Passing through the cemetery gates, her footsteps directed toward home, Buffy wondered idly if the recent increase in numbers of undead rising from their graves meant that Angelus was considering a new tactic: raising his own personal army to help him take on Buffy.

No, she thought wearily. *This is definitely a job he's going to want to finish himself.*

It seemed strange on this otherwise serene spring night that her thoughts were so chilling and bleak. In fact, it was more than strange. It was unfair. Mature as Buffy had become in the last few years, when the weight of the world was placed firmly on her shoulders, there was still a small petulant part of her that from time to time would cry out from the depths, *It's not fair!* Grace had forgiven James for killing both of them when she tried to deny their love. There wasn't a jury in the world that would convict Buffy when the day finally came for her to take Angel's life. But the question of forgiveness plagued her. Was she going to have to forgive Angel before she killed him in order to find some sense of peace? Did she even have the power to forgive him? Or, more importantly, herself?

It wasn't fair.

But in the life of the Slayer, that's just the way it was.

Unlike Buffy, Sunnydale High School freshman Josh Grodin had already finished his weekend homework. This was a good thing, since the last few hours sitting cross-legged on the floor in a circle of his own blood chanting by candlelight had left him exhausted, sweaty, and in no mood to think about algebra.

Josh was raising a demon.

At least that's what he hoped he was doing. It had taken him the better part of six months of hoarding his paper route money to afford the beetle dung, newt eyes, iddlywilde root, and various other strange components the spell required. Had he been forced to also purchase a spell book from the quaint little magic supply shop he'd found in one of Sunnydale's seedier downtown streets, he'd have been a junior before he would have had a chance to make this work, but thankfully, the book in question had been found in the school library tucked between two reference books he'd been seeking about twentieth-century American poetry.

He hadn't bothered to check the book out. The absence of a date stamp tab in the back and a handwritten notation in the front cover indicated that this book was the personal property of the school's quaint British librarian, Mr. Giles. Beggars couldn't be choosers, and though Josh thought of himself as a good, respectable kid, he had quickly thrust the spell book into his backpack the moment he'd found it, only realizing later that this time last year he would never have thought of stealing from the school, or the librarian, let alone had the guts to attempt it.

But then, everything had been different a year ago. Josh had been a good student with a few close friends, as well as a promising forward on the all-city soccer team. His father had been holding down a full-time job as a plumber's assistant, and his mother had been alive.

Three months after Josh's mother had been diagnosed with cancer, she'd gone from the solid place on which his life was centered to a pale shadow of her former self. Alone in his room he had sobbed nightly for what seemed like distant delirious months as his mother teetered on the brink between life and death. At the time, he had believed that was as close to hell as he would ever come in this world, but once she was gone, he had been shocked and sickened to learn that hell had many circles and his mother's death had only granted him access to the first and most mundane.

His father, Robert, had taken his wife's death even

harder than Josh did. What had been in his mother's lifetime a slightly annoying tendency to toss back a few too many beers once in a while with his fellow plumbers had become a daily ritual. It began with the top being popped from the first of at least a case of beer, followed by several bottles of harder stuff that usually left his father in a self-induced comatose state by the wee hours of the night. From this, he would awake midmorning in time to make a quick trip to the nearest liquor store and begin the process again by early afternoon.

Disheartening as the beginning of the process was to watch, and disgusting as the end was to witness each night, the problem was the middle, the hours when Josh usually returned from school or practice to find his father alert and belligerent waiting on the living room sofa to pick a fight.

At first, Josh had tried to understand and be patient. Even when the abuse had escalated from verbal torments to the occasional shove or slap, Josh had reminded himself that his father had to be feeling as bad as he did. Surely, this would pass. But as the weeks turned into months, Josh had slowly come to accept the reality that his mother wasn't the only parent he had lost. The monster that now padded around the house in his father's old pajamas bore no resemblance to the man who had raised him.

Josh was alone and defenseless. He had no idea where to turn. Even the school nurse didn't question him when he told her he'd broken his arm in a skateboarding accident or received that huge black eye from an errant soccer ball. He needed help, and the answer to his prayers had come in the form of a dusty old book and an ancient incantation that would waken the spirit of a demon known as Hector who, the spell promised, would be bound to protect the one who raised him until the end of time.

Josh didn't think it would take that long for his dad to get the message. A few rounds with Hector would surely be enough to make him understand that using his son for a punching bag was no longer an option. Maybe his father would just leave. Josh didn't like to think much about what would come after that. He vaguely imagined himself surviving through the next few years on cereal and TV dinners. But whatever it was, it couldn't possibly be worse than the life he was living right now. Hector would come and save him, and the rest he'd figure out later.

The problem was he'd been chanting the incantation over and over for the better part of five hours, and so far, no Hector.

Josh considered reaching out of the circle to grab the book, which was resting open on his bed only a few feet away, but he worried that breaking the plane of the circle, something the book clearly instructed him not to do once the ritual had begun, might mean he'd have to start again from the beginning, and he didn't think he had that in him. He was also afraid that the blood he had procured by opening a vein in his arm and that had dried some time ago might no longer have the potency required to call the demon.

Resigning himself to continue, he began the chant

again, hoping he wasn't making too much of a mess of the words. He thought they might be Latin but most he could barely pronounce. Then he heard it.

"Josh?"

A guttural growl from down the hall, followed by the sound of kitchen cabinets being slammed open and shut.

"Damn it, Josh!"

Louder.

Next would come the footsteps pounding their way down the hall. Then the incoherent shouting that was meant to communicate the rage his father felt at having already finished his day's supply of whatever had been cheapest when he made his morning Mecca to the mini-mart.

"Where are you?"

Maybe he'd get lucky tonight. Maybe his father would forget that it was Sunday and Josh was home. Maybe his father would trip over his own feet on his way down the hall and pass out for a few more hours somewhere between the kitchen and Josh's bedroom.

Willing himself to remain calm and hold on to some of these happier thoughts, Josh began the incantation again. He could hear his voice rising in fear and panic, but he didn't care. Truth was, the only thing that could save him this night was probably Hector. If he didn't show up soon, all bets would be off.

Suddenly something in the room changed. Josh couldn't be sure it wasn't his imagination, but it seemed that the temperature had dropped severely. The next thing he knew, the black pillar candle he held in his hands and all of the other candles surrounding the circle simultaneously blew out. As a twinge of excitement coursed through his veins, a small speck of bright light appeared at eye level and began to flutter before him. The light grew brighter, then, with a crack, the entire house seemed to shake on its foundation. It was like an earthquake that only lasted a fraction of a second.

In the cold darkness, Josh heard a voice, and it was not at all the voice his imagination had already assigned to Hector.

"Joshua," the voice said, low, but almost sweet, "are you there, dear?"

The bedroom's overhead light flicked on, and Josh turned immediately to face the doorway, where a small, white-haired woman in a pink floral dress with a lace collar and very sensible shoes stood with her hand on the light switch.

"There you are, dear," she said kindly. "Do get up, and let's find a rag to wash that floor. Bloodstains in hardwood can be very difficult to remove, especially when they've had time to set."

Josh had expected to be frightened when Hector appeared. The sight of this woman, whoever she was, did little to instill terror, though her presence and knowledge of whence she must have come did keep Josh riveted to the floor, despite her benign and almost grandmotherly demeanor.

"What are you waiting for?" she asked a little more sternly.

"Who are you?" Josh finally found voice to say.

"I'm Paulina, dearest. But you can call me Polly. All my friends do," she replied.

"I thought, that is, I don't mean to be rude," Josh continued, choosing his words very carefully. "It's just, I was trying to reach Hector," he finished.

"Oh, Hector got out of the protector business years ago. I think he spends most of his time now in that lovely dimension where everything is made of shrimp. Or perhaps it's the one where there is no shrimp. It can be hard to keep track you know."

"B-but . . . ," Josh stammered, unsure how to begin, let alone end the sentence that was forming on his lips. "How can you . . ." The question trailed off.

"Protect you?" Polly replied, her face breaking into a wide and kind of disturbing smile. "You let me worry about that, Josh. And you worry about cleaning up this mess, all right?"

Josh rose from the floor. He couldn't say exactly why, but something in Polly's firm and commanding nature told him that while she might not be the most frightening demon on the block, it probably wouldn't be wise to cross her. The rags and disinfectant he would need to clean the floor were in the kitchen, and he paused before he reached the door, concerned that he would encounter his father between here and there. Polly had busied herself testing the surfaces of his bookcase and footboard for dust as he crossed the room, humming softly under her breath.

"And don't worry about your father," Polly said suddenly, as if she'd been reading his thoughts. "He won't trouble us again."

"What did you do?" Josh asked, suddenly extremely nervous.

"What you wanted," she replied.

Josh shivered involuntarily.

Swallowing his fear, he said simply, "Oh, okay. Thanks."

"You're welcome," Polly said sweetly. "And when you get back, we'll talk about what you're going to do for me."

Josh couldn't be sure why, but something in her tone and words filled him with cold dread. As he opened the door and quickly scanned the hallway, seeing no sign of his father, he silently wished that Hector had been the one to answer his call. His picture in the spell book had been terrifying to behold, but instinctively Josh knew that he would rather have faced a hundred Hectors than one Polly.

Drusilla couldn't sleep. She'd had a very full evening. Hunting in Sunnydale had a particular charm that even months after her arrival had yet to pale. Or perhaps it was just hunting with Angelus again. She had always felt a special bond with him. Of course that was natural between a vampire and their sire. But what she shared with Angelus was something more. He rarely, if ever, hunted merely for the sake of feeding. Had that been the case, any random passerby would have sufficed. Angelus had managed to elevate a simple biological need into poetry. And the past few nights had been particularly gratifying in that regard.

Poor Angelus had been violated. His body had

been invaded by love, and he was determined to purge himself of every last shred of love's painful and disgusting thrall. She would have thought the toddler they had managed to snatch from its weary mother at the bus depot the very night he'd been possessed would have more than satiated his visceral need to bathe in evil. But each night since then he'd continued to ratchet up both the forcefulness and the foulness of his desires. Dru had found herself struggling to keep up, which was absolutely thrilling.

But that wasn't the source of her restlessness. She was troubled by a secret wish she had yet to put into words. Perhaps if she was to share her desires with Angelus, or her longtime lover, Spike, they might subside, but somehow she knew that neither of them, much as they adored her, would have any patience for the scandalous thoughts that refused to give her a moment's peace.

Drusilla had been toying with the idea for weeks now, ever since she, Angelus, and Spike had moved from the factory to the abandoned mansion on the outskirts of Sunnydale that they now called home. The mansion had needed work when they first arrived, most of which they had already accomplished. Though they spent much of their time in the spacious den, whose most impressive feature was a vast fireplace, or bathing in the moonlight that fell into the first-floor courtyard, the main floor's master bedroom, which they had transformed with deep red velvet curtains and a massive four-poster eighteenth-century bed, had become Dru's favorite room in the house.

Only a few days after they had arrived, however, she had made her way through the second floor of the east wing.

Three large bedrooms took up most of the space, but at the end of the hall, Dru had discovered a playroom. She could smell the remnants of many happy hours spent here by the children for whom the room had been built. It left her faintly nauseated. But at the same time, there was a tangible thrill to it.

Her first thought upon entering the brightly colored room was to wonder if its former occupants had had any sense of how lucky they were to have had such a room at their disposal, or how she would have treasured the opportunity to enter the room while the children played and descend upon each of them, one at a time, filling their tiny souls with terror before they succumbed to the darkness that would be her final gift to them.

But the thought that halted her in her tracks, and kept her awake these many nights hence, had come second. She found herself wondering why, in all the years she had spent roaming the world, it had never occurred to her. Since her new life as a vampire had begun, she had known all manner of vampires and demons. She had ruthlessly treasured every moment spent playing vile games and making new conquests with her beloved Spike and Angelus. They belonged to one another in a way that no living person could ever comprehend and with a dark depth that was both rich and satisfying. But neither Spike nor Angelus actually needed Drusilla; not the way the children for whom this playroom had been built had needed their parents or their siblings. Drusilla had been desired in life and adored in death. But had she ever been needed?

There was only one answer before her. It both tantalized and terrified her. Something buried deep within her was actually vaguely repulsed by the thought, which in and of itself made it worth exploring more deeply.

In her secret, no longer beating heart of hearts, Drusilla had decided she wanted someone to love and need her in a way that neither Spike nor Angelus could ever imagine.

Drusilla wanted a child of her own.

Chapter Two

Buffy was a firm believer in the two-and-a-half-day weekend. In fact, she wouldn't have found any strong moral objection to a three-, four-, or five-day weekend, come to think of it. If she ever ruled the world, that would certainly be one of the first agenda items she would propose. In the meantime, she was almost as pleased as most of her fellow students that they'd been given Monday morning off and would start this short school week on Monday afternoon. It was a blessing, and such little gifts from the universe were rare enough in the life of a vampire slayer. It wasn't world peace, but she'd take what she could get.

Why the teachers of Sunnydale would be required to have an "In-Service" day so close to the end of a school year, Buffy couldn't imagine. Perhaps it had something to do with the extremely paranormal makeover the school had received the previous week when the ghosts who possessed Buffy and Angel had been running rampant. It was possible that mysterious locker monsters, staircase landings that turned to quicksand, and plagues of wasps hadn't been as easy to recover from as the more tame adventures of the school's past, for instance, possessed students that ate their principal for lunch.

Sometimes Buffy was grateful that she had been given the power to fight the world's demons. But more often than not, as she passed small groups of students relaxing on the school's sun-drenched front lawn before fourth period trading reviews of the movies they'd seen that weekend, Buffy wished that she were as blissfully ignorant as most of her peers. She vaguely remembered what it was like to live in a world that made sense, a world where the monsters under your bed at night were vanquished by nothing more than a reassuring parent's smile and a glass of warm milk, a world where a girl was more concerned about which color nail polish was "in" this spring than how to get demon blood out of a favorite tank top.

Unfortunately, being the "Chosen One" was a one-way deal. No one had considered whether or not Buffy *wanted* the job when she was called to be the Slayer. And strangely, knowing all she now did, even she could not say for certain whether or not she would have embraced her calling or refused it, had the "Chosen" part included any input from the "choose-ee."

At the very least, she had to be grateful that she wasn't the only student at Sunnydale High who was painfully aware that things that went bump in the night were real and usually kind of smelly. Spotting Willow Rosenberg, a petite redhead curled into a corner of the student lounge sofa, head buried in a book as usual, Buffy quickly darted through the early morning hallway traffic and grabbed the open seat next to her best friend.

"Is that how those book thingies work?" Buffy asked as she tossed her own pile of texts onto the table before her. "You have to open them to get the prize?"

"Oh, hey, Buffy," Willow replied without lifting her gaze.

Gently rebuked, Buffy considered her friend. Willow was easily one of the smartest people she'd ever met. And usually she managed very well not to flaunt her intellectual superiority in the faces of those less fortunate, including Buffy. In fact, her truly sweet and generous nature had been one of the first things that had drawn Buffy to seek out Willow's friendship—that and Buffy's need to not fail out of Sunnydale High within a few days of her arrival on campus. Although Buffy could not have known it at the time, the nerdlike surface that had caused so many to overlook Willow for so long had merely been the delicate facade that shrouded the strongest heart and most courageous spirit Buffy had ever encountered. Despite Willow's sensitivities, including frog fear, Buffy was more grateful than she could ever express that Willow had chosen to stand beside her in her fiercest battles, lending incredible moral support, along with enviable research skills to the Slayer's missions.

It was therefore vaguely unsettling that Willow seemed to be leaning toward the mopes this early in the day. Buffy decided to move on to a topic toward which even grumpy Willow would warm.

"How was the In-Service this morning? Have your fellow faculty members shared with you the power to give detentions yet?" Buffy asked.

"What? Oh, sure," Willow replied, still not really giving her full attention to Buffy.

"All right, Wil, what gives?" Buffy replied a bit more tersely. "It's the beginning of a school day. Granted, it's a short day, but usually that's cause for joy in the land of Willow."

"I'm sorry," Willow replied, closing her book and gracing Buffy with a faint smile.

Suddenly, Buffy regretted her choice of topic. True, Willow seemed to be enjoying her new position as temporary teacher in the computer science lab. But Willow had only accepted the job upon the untimely death of the regular teacher, Jenny Calendar. Ms. Calendar had been more than a teacher. She'd been warming the heart of Buffy's Watcher, Mr. Giles, and was a gypsy spy sent by her people to watch over Angel. It had taken Buffy some serious in-the-moment maturing to make some sort of peace with Ms. Calendar once she learned that she wasn't just hanging out with Giles and occasionally helping Buffy solve whatever crisis was at hand out of the goodness of her heart. But nothing Ms. Calendar had done had warranted the brutality with which Angel had snapped her neck, and even weeks later, the loss was still fresh among all who had known her, particularly Willow and Giles.

"No, Willow," Buffy began. "My bad. It's not anything to joke about."

"No. 'A' for effort, really," Willow replied. "It's just, I didn't get to go to the In-Service."

"What happened?"

"It's nothing," Willow said hesitantly.

"Wil, that's not your 'nothing' face. That's your 'something' face. Actually, it's your 'this is really something and I don't think I want Buffy to know about it' face."

"It's no biggie," Willow replied. "Mom was doing a little spring cleaning on Sunday and found that crucifix we nailed to my wall when we were doing the spell to un-invite Angel."

"Oh," Buffy said, absolutely certain that there was no way this story ended well.

"So there was talking and a little crying and a call to Rabbi 911," Willow continued.

"How bad is it?" Buffy asked.

"They're thinking about sending me to a kibbutz this summer, but I think I can get out of it. Maybe Giles knows a spell," Willow suggested, brightening just a bit.

"I'm sorry, Wil," Buffy said quickly. "It's my fault."

"No, it absolutely is not," Willow said defiantly. "I was the one who invited Angel into my room in the first place."

"You had no reason not to at the time," Buffy interjected.

"And you had no reason to think any of the rest of it would happen either," Willow insisted. "I didn't want to tell you because you already have enough to worry about. It's nothing, really," she finished, doing her best to smile. "And you're right. It's just the beginning of another fun-filled week at Sunnydale High. How bad could it be?"

"You're not seriously asking that question?" Buffy replied.

"No, I guess not," Willow said thoughtfully.

Their musings were interrupted by the sound of Principal Snyder shouting at the top of his lungs, "Who did it? Who thinks this blatant display of disrespect is amusing?"

The friends turned in unison to see the troll of a man who had been terrorizing Sunnydale High since last spring marching down the main hallway, stopping at every cluster of students he encountered to check hands and bags and to hand out detentions at the slightest smirks in his direction.

"Sounds like someone hasn't had their coffee yet." Buffy smiled. It was impossible for her not to hate the man who had gone out of his way since they'd first met to remind Buffy that she was a delinquent and that he would relish the chance to expel her given the slightest provocation.

"Oh, how cute," Willow said, offering the first genuine smile Buffy had seen from her all day and pointing in Snyder's general direction.

"Did you just use the word 'cute' in reference to Snyder?" Buffy asked in disbelief, following her friend's gaze. It only took a moment to see what was wrong with the picture before her. The principal was wearing only one shoe. His left foot was clad in a baby pink argyle sock. Given Willow's eclectic fashion sense, Buffy no longer had any difficulty understanding her friend's reaction.

"Fun as this is to watch, I should really check in with Giles before fourth period," Buffy said, collecting her books and rising from the couch.

"Is anything wrong?" Willow asked with sudden seriousness. "How was your weekend, by the way?"

"Oh, you know," Buffy replied as both moved gingerly toward the main hall, careful to avoid Snyder's scrutiny. "I hung out at the mall, took in a few movies, got a manicure, and Mom sprung for this really cute bag I've had my eye on."

"Really?" Willow asked in obvious disbelief.

"Sure," Buffy replied, "in the *Fantasy Island* version of my life. In reality, our undead friends were out in full force, and I broke the last two nails I had dusting some newbie named Brower. He wasn't all that strong, but he was fast."

"Oh," Willow said sadly. "Conrad Brower?"

"I think so," Buffy replied, trying to remember the full name on the headstone.

"He was my ophthalmologist," Willow said.

"You don't even wear glasses. Why do you need an ophthalmologist?"

"You can't neglect the health of your eyes," Willow replied. "Everyone should have their eyes examined at least once a year. And he gave out these yummy butterscotch lollipops with each exam."

They had almost reached the library, Willow continuing to opine about the dearth of really good butterscotch, when Giles emerged from the double doors that separated his haven from the rest of the school. A vision in tweed, Giles was Buffy's Watcher, appointed by a council in England to train and mentor the Slayer.

"Ah, good morning, Buffy, Willow," Giles said cordially.

"Hi, Giles," Willow said cheerfully.

"I'm so glad to have run into you before class," Giles continued.

"Cut to the chase, Giles," Buffy replied warily. "Who's trying to destroy the world this week?"

"Oh, no one, actually," Giles said evenly.

"Really?" Buffy asked, a faint note of hope creeping into her voice.

"Yes," Giles continued. "All is quiet on the Hellmouth. At least, for the moment."

"That's what I like to hear," Buffy said. "Maybe I'll actually make it to a few classes today."

"Indeed," Giles replied. "Though there was one rather disturbing disappearance reported in the weekend papers."

"I knew it was too good to last," Buffy countered.

"It's probably not demon-related, though, of course, one never knows," Giles went on. "An eight-year-old girl, Callie McKay, was reported missing from the park. Her parents are quite beside themselves with worry."

"And upsetting as that is," Buffy retorted, "unless

she was kidnapped by a demon, it's not my responsibility, right? I mean, the Sunnydale police force does get to solve a crime once in a while, don't they?"

"Of course, such as they are," Giles replied.

"Good," Buffy finished. "Now, if you'll excuse me, I have a chemistry quiz to fail."

As Willow was required to be home immediately after school that day, and Xander, Buffy's other best friend, was doing his best to make her want to take her own life by openly reveling in his new relationship with their fr-enemy Cordelia, Buffy actually arrived home from school rather early for a change. She was first shocked, then dismayed, when she popped into the kitchen to make a quick snack and found her mother seated at the counter, her face etched with worry and her foot shaking up and down expectantly.

"Hey, Mom," Buffy said cautiously, wondering why at-will invisibility wasn't one of her Slayer powers. Joyce Summers ran a local art gallery, and there were very few things that would bring the concerned small-business owner home before dinnertime. "Shouldn't you be gallery girl, or art girl, right now?" Buffy asked, opening the fridge.

"I should," Joyce replied. "Instead, I had children."

Uh-oh, Buffy thought.

"Principal Snyder called me at work today," Joyce said ponderously.

"I didn't steal his shoe," Buffy said quickly.

"What?" Joyce asked.

"Never mind," Buffy replied. "What did he want?"

"He wanted to make sure I was aware that your finals are coming up."

"Has there been a rash of calendar thefts?" Buffy asked. "School ends in, like, three weeks. Who doesn't know that finals are coming up?"

"He also wanted to make sure that I was aware that you are currently barely scraping up passing grades in history and English lit, and are actually failing chemistry. Apparently, unless you perform at a level that he is fairly certain is unattainable for you, you will not be spending your senior year at Sunnydale High. You'll be repeating your junior year at another school."

This was hardly a new theme in the Summers house. Buffy's grades had never been the best, but they had certainly been good enough to avoid parental scrutiny—until she had been called to slay vampires. The cold, hard reality was that saving the world often cut into valuable study time, and though Buffy did her best at school, in the last couple of years her best had become seriously underwhelming in the grade department. Since Joyce was unaware of her daughter's status as the Chosen One, Buffy couldn't actually make her understand that the fact that she attended school at all was cause for celebration. Sighing deeply, Buffy put on her bravest face and said, "Not to worry, Mom. Willow and I are on the study wagon. My chemistry exam is more than half of my final grade, and I'm already doing practice essays for English."

Shaking her head, Joyce replied, "You and Willow do nothing but 'study.' All hours of the day and night you are always at the library or with Willow, supposedly studying."

This was as far from the truth as it was possible to get, but Buffy was unfortunately unable to share with Joyce the reality that "study time" had become the convenient parental code word for fighting vampires and demons. Any time spent in the school library was either about honing her slaying skills with Giles or reading up in some dusty tome about whomever or whatever had just rolled into town determined to permanently remove the sun from Sunnydale. Buffy rued the fact that she would never be tested on the history of ancient vampires, the mating habits of giant praying mantises, or the hatching cycles of Bezor demons. Those exams Buffy had aced, though they would never appear on her transcript or help her GPA.

As Buffy reveled in the unfairness of it all, Joyce continued: "Principal Snyder tells me you've been placed in a special category of academic probation."

"Principal Snyder hates me," Buffy said truthfully.

"Be that as it may, your record has been brought before the school board, and they've recommended a special tutor for you."

"But, Mom!" Buffy whined.

"You'll meet with him four times a week until finals," Joyce finished, giving no ground for argument.

"Starting when?" Buffy asked, clearly dismayed.

"Tonight," Joyce replied firmly.

Buffy had already planned a night at the Bronze, followed by a sweep of two of the local cemeteries for the evening's festivities, but it was clear from her mother's face that her foot was firmly in the down position. One of the things that made Buffy's life bearable was her mother's seemingly endless capacity to make allowances for the strange things that surrounded her daughter without asking too many questions. The parenting manuals that had occupied most of Joyce's bookshelves since her daughter had been expelled from her previous high school for burning down the school gymnasium (it had been filled with vampires at the time) all told her that teenagers needed space as well as understanding, and Joyce had given Buffy more than enough of both. But Buffy knew that her mother could only be pushed so far. Deciding that "dutiful daughter" was the card to play here, Buffy acquiesced, saying only, "Tonight. Perfect. Thanks, Mom."

Two hours and several desperate but fruitless phone calls to Willow, Xander, and Giles later, Buffy heard the doorbell ring and with a heavy heart and leaden feet made her way to the staircase landing to meet her doom.

She was totally unprepared for the sight of her tutor, a boy who couldn't have been more than twenty, with casually disheveled brown hair and truly striking green eyes.

"Good evening, Ms. Summers," he said, politely shaking her mother's hand as he entered the front hall. "I'm Todd Harter. I'm here to work with Buffy."

"It's nice to meet you, Todd," Joyce was saying calmly as Buffy found herself wondering who in the world had just sucked all the oxygen out of the room.

She couldn't remember the last time she had had

such a visceral reaction to the cuteness of a boy. Actually, she could. It had taken place a year and a half earlier, the night Angel had walked into her life with his brooding good looks, cryptic warnings, and his first gift to her, a silver crucifix she now had a hard time wearing without regret.

Thankfully, the minute she connected the feeling she was currently experiencing with Angel, it lost some of its potency. There had never been a love that had come with a higher price tag than hers and Angel's, and Buffy had decided weeks ago that the words "Never Again" were going to be etched on her tombstone.

It was just hard to keep that in mind as Todd walked calmly up the stairs and, reaching out his hand with a genuine and perfect smile, said, "I sure hope you're Buffy."

Spike was debating a night on the town with his beloved Dru—*Where the hell is she, by the way?*—when the front door of the mansion was thrown open and Angel swept in, unceremoniously dropped a frail-looking man at Spike's wheels, and said casually, "I thought you might like some leftovers for dinner."

Cringing at the overwhelming rankness wafting from the body of the man lying prostrate before him, Spike swallowed the nauseating bile that had started to boil within him almost every time Angel spoke and quipped, "What, the streets of Sunnyhell were all out of anemics tonight?"

"Buggers can't be choosers," Angel tossed over his

shoulder as he disappeared into the mansion's court-yard.

Spike knew full well that Angel's apparent largesse was nothing more than a backhanded reminder that Spike hadn't been at full strength for months. He had been severely injured in a church fire during one of many perfect plans the Slayer had turned to crap. A ceremony meant to kill the old soul-filled Angel and cure Drusilla of her illness had ended in flames and near death. Difficult as it was to believe, he and Angel were now at even more deeply entrenched cross-purposes than when Angel was doing time as the Slayer's lapdog. Back in the days when Angelus, Darla, Spike, and Dru had cut a fearsome and bloody swath through most of Europe and Asia, Spike would never have guessed that a friendship such as theirs, forged in blood, could have come to this. But Angel had changed. Or maybe Spike had. Either way, his old friend was now a wanker of the worst sort, and Spike only longed to be rid of him.

Still, dinner was dinner. Nudging the still form at his feet with the tip of his boot, Spike rolled the man over and was rewarded by a hefty stench of sweat and Thunderbird for his trouble. *Not if you were the last meal on legs,* Spike decided, realizing that Angel hadn't fed off the vagrant either, probably for the same reasons that had turned Spike's stomach. Whatever blood was left in the man was so poisoned by years of deprivation and a diet of cheap wine that Spike would have tasted it for weeks. At this point, he wasn't even sure if setting the man on fire right then and there would be enough to get the stench out of the carpet.

These bleak thoughts were quickly dispelled by a gentle sound coming from the direction of the front door.

"The stars and the moon, the dark and the gloom," Drusilla was singing softly as she made her way up the front walk. Though Spike didn't like to think of Dru and Angel hunting together—*Hell, I don't like to think of the two of them watching the telly together*—at least the light of his life was finally home. Spike allowed his mind to drift to thoughts of the painful and satisfying games they would play once they had retired to the master bedroom at sunrise.

His joyful anticipation was only heightened when Spike caught his first glimpse of his beloved, her long black fur-trimmed coat barely concealing the blood-red gown that he'd found for her on their last visit to Paris, its plunging neckline gloriously accentuating the perfection of her pure white skin. As if that vision were not enough to set his flesh tingling, Dru was gently guiding a beautiful young girl with golden curls, clad in a frilly pink jumper, toward him, holding one of the child's hands with the tips of her perfectly manicured nails.

"Now this is more like it, pet," Spike cooed lovingly. "To what do I owe this incredible generosity? I know the young are your favorite. Did you actually save this little bit for me?"

"Patience, love," Dru replied, bending to whisper in the child's ear.

Savoring the anticipation of the delectable morsel

to come, Spike wheeled himself a bit closer, stopping in horror only when the little girl's face suddenly transformed into that of a vampire.

"Callie," Dru whispered softly, "say hello to your new daddy, Spike."

"Oh, sodding hell," Spike sputtered.

Chapter Three

Monday's soccer practice had not gone well for Josh. He didn't know if he was more distracted or exhausted, and the extra mile Coach Bradley had demanded he run at the end of the afternoon had done nothing to improve the situation. As much as he dreaded returning home, by nightfall, he had little choice.

Making his way through the backyard to his kitchen door, Josh slowed his steps, lost for a moment in the pleasant memory of a spring afternoon he'd spent picking grapefruit from his mother's favorite tree that dominated much of the yard. Somewhere in his distant past were gentle days when his mother had lifted him in her arms and allowed him to choose a fruit, tickling him as the sweet, tangy pink grapefruit juice ran down his chin. Tonight he could see that the tree was one of the few things in the backyard that hadn't died, though it was well past time to trim it back, and fruits in varying stages of decomposition littered the ground beneath it.

Josh turned again toward the back door, and as he did so, something assaulted his senses, threatening to drive him even further into his past. It wasn't the tree, or the yard. Instead, it was a smell that wafted through the open kitchen window, à rich aroma that set his stomach rumbling.

Somewhere, just beyond the door he so feared to open, was a home-cooked dinner.

Alert and anxious, Josh entered the kitchen and his eyes confirmed what his nose suspected. The small Formica table was set for two, and steaming dishes of mashed potatoes and mixed vegetables sat beside a freshly roasted chicken, still on the bone and ready for carving.

Without thought, Josh dropped his backpack and jammed his finger into the potatoes for a taste, but before he could bring that finger to his lips, a shrill "Joshua, what do you think you're doing?" met his ears and he instinctively pulled both of his hands behind his back and turned to face Polly, who was busy removing a tray of freshly baked dinner rolls from the oven.

"I'm sorry," he stammered.

"Sorry doesn't cream the corn," Polly replied sharply. "You will wash your filthy hands and face and put those foul-smelling clothes in the laundry room before you enjoy so much as a crumb from this table. Do you understand?" she finished.

"Yes, ma'am," Josh replied automatically, before adding apologetically, "Everything smells great."

"Of course it does, dear." Polly smiled warmly. "Now move!"

Josh found himself hurrying to do her bidding, unable to believe his good fortune. Hector might have been his first choice in a protector, but he doubted the mammoth demon would have known his way around a kitchen, or a vacuum cleaner, he mentally added, realizing as he made his way down the hall that the house was the cleanest it had been in over a year. His room smelled of fresh pine and lemon. The starched and ironed pillowcases atop his perfectly made bed and the ordered arrangement of his books and soccer trophies on his desk all testified to the fact that Polly had made herself more than useful during the day. He rejoiced inwardly at the knowledge that when he presented himself at her table—*funny how the entire house now seems to belong to her*—he would do so with something to offer her by way of thanks.

It hadn't been easy. In fact, it had been terrifying, but Josh had managed to accomplish the only thing Polly had asked of him in return for her protection that very afternoon at school.

Josh had stolen Principal Snyder's shoe.

He would never have been able to manage it without specific instructions from Polly the night before as to how exactly he might accomplish this minor miracle. It had depended upon two things. The first was the existence of a small faculty bathroom just down the hall from the principal's office that Snyder had immediately designated for his exclusive use once he had joined the administration of Sunnydale High. Though few faculty members seemed to genuinely like the principal, ever fewer seemed willing to risk his displeasure on any given day, so the rest of the faculty had given up this small privilege without too many complaints. The second was an odd personal habit of Snyder's. Apparently, whenever the principal retired to his private domain and entered the bathroom's only stall, he removed his shoes and placed them on the floor in front of him before he sat down. This, Polly had assured him, he had done ever since he was a little boy.

Josh's heart had been in his throat as he had silently entered the bathroom that afternoon, a good forty-five minutes before the bell was to ring. But just as Polly had said, he had seen Principal Snyder's polished black dress shoes poking out from the stall door, and he was out of the bathroom, shoe in bag, and well down the hall before he had heard the first shriek of alarm from the principal echoing behind him.

Now that the deed had been accomplished, and fortified by the prospect of the most delicious meal he'd had in a year as a reward, Josh re-entered the kitchen a few minutes later with a spring in his step and the slightly ripe dress shoe in his hand.

Polly turned immediately to face him upon his return, and he reveled at the glimmer of satisfaction in her eyes as he approached her, holding the shoe before him like a holy relic.

"Oh, my dear, dear boy," Polly cooed warmly. "Well, done."

"You're welcome," Josh replied as she quickly plucked the shoe from his hands and clutched it to her heart, regarding it with almost the same affection a mother would have for a newborn child.

"Do sit down and eat something," Polly said absently, still cradling the shoe.

"Thank you, ma'am," Josh answered, and immediately sat and began to pile his plate with as much fresh food as it would hold.

The first bite of potatoes had barely touched his tongue when a wave of nausea tightened his gut. As Polly took her place beside him, setting the shoe in her lap, she seemed to notice his attempt to force down the food.

"Is everything all right, dear?" she asked with genuine concern.

"Oh, yes," Josh replied as best he could, though he hesitated to fill another forkful.

The potatoes tasted so foul, he could barely swallow them. He didn't know if they had been rank before she had cooked them, or if she had mashed them with sour milk. In any event, they were inedible. He turned his attention to the chicken, hoping for something better. Though his appetite had gone with the first of the potatoes, in his limited experience there was little harm that could be done to a freshly roasted chicken.

Like the potatoes, however, the first bite of chicken was also to be his last.

"Eat up, dear," Polly was saying as she filled her own plate. "You're a growing boy, and you need your nutrition."

The meat assaulted his taste buds with a riot of decay and rot that he could only associate with a cat that had once died in his backyard. It had been found several days too late to do anything about the smell but wait it out.

"Is there a problem, dear?" Polly asked sweetly as Josh instinctively spat the chicken back onto his plate and dropped his fork.

"No, ma'am," Josh replied feebly. "I guess I'm just not as hungry as I thought."

"I spent the entire afternoon preparing this meal, Joshua," Polly began sternly, "and you will finish every bite of it before you leave this table."

Josh looked at the plate, then at Polly, and took a moment to evaluate where the greater threat lay.

Unfortunately, he chose wrong.

"I have a history paper to write," he said as he began to rise from the table.

"What did you say, young man?" Polly asked, standing as well and suddenly taking on a more menacing appearance than he would ever have thought possible in floral cotton and lace.

"I-I . . . ," Josh started to stammer.

"Boys."

Polly spat the word as if it tasted as bad to her as the chicken had tasted to Josh.

"Just like my Cecil," she began. "You're all the same: ungrateful and selfish. You don't understand a mother's love, and you have no respect for the time and energy it takes to care for pathetic little wretches like you," Polly continued.

Josh stepped back from the table, and found his back against the kitchen wall. His hand started to move of its own accord down the length of the wall until it found the knob to the basement door. As Polly continued her rant, flecks of spittle flying from her lips along with insults, Josh threw open the door and, as quickly as he could, rushed down the basement steps.

Polly followed him to the doorway, the pitch of her voice rising until her words became unintelligible shrieks, and Josh quickly realized he had all but cornered himself. As he searched for a defensible position, he noted for the first time in the shadows cast by the basement's single overhanging bulb a hand reaching out to him from the far corner, nearest what had been his father's workbench.

"Dad?" Josh whispered.

As Polly began to descend the steps, Joshua reached for the hand only to find that it was ice cold to his touch, and much lighter than it should have been. This made immediate sense when he tugged on the hand, only to find that while it was still connected to his father's forearm, the rest of his father was no longer attached to it.

"What did you do?" Joshua screamed, turning on Polly, who now stood, arms crossed, at the base of the stairs.

"I did what you asked," Polly replied evenly. "Your father will never hurt you again."

"I . . . I . . ." But Josh couldn't finish the thought. Much as he had hated his father, much as his father had made his life a living hell over the past year, Josh was completely unprepared for his dismemberment. Josh no longer knew what exactly he had wanted when he had summoned Polly. All he knew for sure was that he hadn't wanted *this*.

Mustering all the courage that remained in him, Josh turned to Polly and shouted, "And I stole that shoe for you! We're even. Now get out!"

Polly seemed to have collected herself. She only smiled slightly at his words.

"I will, dear," she said simply, "just as soon as I've finished cleaning up this mess."

"What mess?" Josh asked. "This house has never been so clean."

"The mess you make by your presence, my boy," Polly replied.

The next thing Josh knew, the hand that still held his father's cold, dead arm felt as if it were on fire. It was almost a pleasant release as the fire subsided, despite the fact that his hand had been pulled from its place on his arm and fell to the floor, alongside his father's arm, with a splat.

The rest of his joints were tingling and beginning to burn when Josh realized just how big a mistake he had made. The last thought he had before the darkness took him was simply, *I'm so sorry,* but he died long before he knew for whom exactly that apology had been meant.

Buffy entered the library Tuesday morning before the start of classes to find Giles standing over Xander, who was seated at the central research table, intently studying what appeared to be an ancient manuscript of some kind. Cordelia stood by, anxiously tapping her foot in a manner that suggested in no uncertain terms she would rather be anywhere but there.

"So is there any way to reach this dimension?" Xander asked seriously.

"It would be most unwise," was Giles's characteristic response.

"But if that's where all my extra socks are—oh, hey, Buffy." Xander interrupted himself, his eyes brightening at the sight of the Slayer.

"Geez, Xander," Cordelia interjected wearily, "if the sock demons—"

"Gnomes," Giles couldn't help but correct her.

"Whatever," Cordelia continued, "if these guys love your socks so much, I say let it go. That's why somebody out there created Target."

"We're talking about a crime against humanity," Xander argued back. "To take one sock at a time, leaving a man with dozens of mismatched pairs—that's just evil."

"Do I need to be here for this?" Buffy asked, stifling a yawn.

Giles busied himself rebinding the manuscript as he answered, "Not at all. Xander was just curious about this rather common phenomenon of seeming to misplace one sock each time one does a load of laundry, and I was attempting to explain—"

"Yeah, we got it," Cordelia interrupted, checking her watch. "Xander has angered the sock gods. Can we go now?"

"Gnomes," Giles added weakly.

"You could show a little compassion," Xander rebuked her. "We don't all have access to your daddy's credit cards, you know."

The very thought of her purchasing power brought a faint smile to Cordelia's lips.

"How was your patrol last night, Buffy?" Giles asked in an obvious effort to change the subject.

"I think he's trying to kill me," she replied, settling for a moment in an open chair and again placing her hand over her mouth to cover a larger yawn.

"Who?" Giles asked, instantly alert. "A demon? A vampire?"

"Angel?" Cordelia added. "'Cause we all knew that."

"My tutor," Buffy replied pointedly. Though she had always known it would be inappropriate to use her powers as a Slayer to harm a human being, there were days—and this was one of them—when she honestly wondered if Cordelia really met that requirement.

"Ah, I see," Giles said thoughtfully. "Terribly demanding, is he?"

"Did you know that King George the Third of England, the guy who was supposedly running your country during the American Revolution, was actually insane?" Buffy asked.

"In fact, I did," Giles replied.

"Or that by the time World War One broke out, most of the monarchs of the various countries that went to war were actually related to one another?"

"Yes, I'm sure I read that somewhere too," Giles continued evenly.

"Well, now I do too," Buffy replied, "along with about fifty other useless facts that I'm going to need to discuss on my world history final, and will be quizzed on tonight, right after I finish my practice essay on the use of metaphor in 'Ode on a Grecian Vase.'"

"Urn," Giles corrected her.

"I thought it was a vase," Buffy said.

"It is, it—never mind. While I'm pleased to see that you're making progress in your studies, I must caution you that this is no time to neglect your slaying duties."

"Like there's any way I don't know that?" Buffy said sharply. Before Giles could retort she added more gently, "I'm sorry. I'm just really tired. I didn't sleep very well last night, and until finals are done, I have my regular homework, plus lots and lots of extra homework."

"Can't Willow be of some assistance?" Giles asked.

"Unless Willow can somehow take my finals and hers at the same time, I'd say no," Buffy replied, then added, "I promise I'll patrol tonight, right after my study session."

"And after that, you should join us at the Bronze," Xander suggested. "Dingoes are playing tonight. Should be happening."

"Yes, well, whatever your plans, do make sure—" Giles began.

"I will. Chosen one. Destiny. Got it," Buffy cut

him off, collecting her books and joining Xander and Cordelia as they made their way to the doors. "Why do they say there's no rest for the wicked? Boy, did they get that one wrong."

She didn't need to turn around to know that Giles was looking after her both concerned and resigned. The truth was, he knew that being the Slayer and a high school junior was no picnic, but there was little he could do at such times to ease her burdens.

As Buffy, Xander, and Cordelia merged into the early morning hallway traffic, Xander picked up on his earlier theme.

"So how about it, Buffy? Up for a little fun tonight?"

"I don't think so, Xander," she replied. "I really have to hit the books tonight. Come to think of it, if hitting them was all I had to do—"

"What's up with him?" Cordelia interrupted.

Buffy and Xander followed her gaze and found she was watching Principal Snyder walk serenely past them, seemingly oblivious to the students around him and the many opportunities for detentions in his wake.

"He looks almost . . ."

"Happy?" Xander finished for Cordelia.

"He probably just saw my score on that chemistry quiz yesterday," Buffy said sadly.

"Oh, what's the big deal," Cordelia said frankly, obviously trying to raise Buffy's spirits in her own special way. "I mean, it's not like you're ever going to need chemistry."

"I will if I want to graduate," Buffy replied.

"Assuming you live that long," Cordelia added.

"Cordelia—" Buffy began.

"That's my girl," Xander said firmly, placing himself between Cordelia and the Slayer, "always trying to find the silver lining."

"I'm just saying . . . ," Cordelia trailed off as he grasped her by the elbow and steered her away from Buffy's frowning face.

"Catch you later, Buffy. And think about tonight. Should be fun!" Xander babbled before saying more quietly to Cordelia, "Sweetie, how many times do we have to talk about quiet, inside thoughts?"

For the moment, Buffy decided to let it go. Truth was, Cordelia had a point. And much as she hated to admit it, she'd often wondered herself how important it was to be a good student, given the life expectancy of the average Slayer.

"So, basically they get all tweaked just because they weren't into queens?"

Ah, Buffy.

Angelus couldn't help but adore the way her mind worked. In fact, the subject had occupied most of his waking and sleeping hours for the better part of the past several weeks. This evening, as he perched outside her bedroom window observing her study session and her new tutor, Angelus fought the temptation to swoop inside and literally drink it in. Of course that would have been impossible, given the fact that he no longer had an invitation to enter Buffy's home, though Angelus doubted that minor obstacle would stop him for long. After a moment he forced himself to focus again on Buffy's conversation.

"No. They liked queens. They usually came with kings as kind of a matched set. But they didn't like the idea that the queen would actually inherit the kingdom."

Then there was *Todd.*

Angelus didn't know Todd. He didn't get the impression that Buffy knew him very well either. But, clearly—and this was the troubling part, or the happy accident, depending on how he chose to look at it—Buffy seemed to like Todd, or at least respect him.

The tutor was still speaking. "Despite the fact that Henry the First specifically stated before his death that his only surviving child, his daughter, Matilda, should succeed him, the nobility of what was really a very young Britain at the time had never been ruled by a woman, and most of them were terribly disconcerted by the idea."

"So this Stephen guy, even though, he's, like, her cousin, and also swore to protect her, turns on her the minute her father dies?" Buffy asked.

"Basically, yeah," Todd answered.

"Typical," Buffy said, rolling her eyes.

And there's the smile.

Angelus had been watching Buffy's study session and her new study partner since sundown. And *Todd,* as that little smile seemed to confirm, was just beginning to realize that there was definitely a whole lot more to the petite blonde with the dusky hazel eyes and the short attention span than one might assume at first glance.

"Why typical?" Todd asked.

"Men in general," Buffy replied curtly.

"I see," Todd said thoughtfully.

That's right, big guy, she's been hurt. Recently. And it's going to take more than that crooked smile and a big brain to make her forget it. In fact . . . she's never going to forget it, if I have anything to say about it.

"So men aren't your favorite subject these days?" Todd asked just innocently enough.

To her credit, Buffy caught the faint whiff of flirtation immediately.

That's my girl.

But then she turned to Todd and, instead of taking the perfect opportunity he had given her to wax rhapsodic about men and their inconstancy, she softened a bit and said, "Not all men, I guess."

"Well, that's good to hear," Todd replied with a bigger smile. "I mean, I can't speak for all men, but for me . . . I guess . . . well, I haven't had a lot of time for . . ."

"What?" Buffy asked, seeming genuinely interested.

Angelus didn't like where this was starting to go one bit.

"It's just, I work pretty hard. Always have. You know . . . I'm trying to put myself through college, but money's pretty tight, so I've got a couple of part-time jobs."

"You mean you're not spending your evenings tutoring the less intellectually inclined just out of the goodness of your heart?" Buffy teased.

"No, I mean, I like tutoring . . ." Todd began.

"It's okay," Buffy chuckled. "I can relate."

"You work part-time too?" Todd asked.

"Not exactly," Buffy replied a little evasively. "I guess the 'never having enough time' part just sounds familiar."

"Oh." Todd nodded. "You're probably pretty busy at school," he suggested. "And I bet you're really popular."

Buffy laughed dismissively. "Then you'd lose."

"Now you're teasing me."

"Nope. I mean, I have friends, good friends, but being popular takes the kind of effort I don't usually have to spare," Buffy said.

"So what do you like to do that takes up so much time?" Todd asked with serious interest.

Angelus watched as Buffy considered her response. No one who didn't know her as well as he would have questioned the sweet mask of innocence that she'd worn through their entire exchange. On the surface, everything about Buffy definitely suggested what Todd was seeing. She was beautiful, funny, and terribly charming. She had "cheerleader" and "homecoming queen" written all over her. And before she'd been called to slay vampires, that, and the mall, had been the sum total of her existence. But now, that beguiling sweetness was tempered by a wealth of experiences, both dark and powerful, at which Todd could never guess. And the reality was, for a man to truly know Buffy, he had to get past the candy shell and dig for the gooey center. That was where the truly good stuff was, and that was the part of her that Angelus was determined to destroy before he allowed himself the exquisite pleasure of killing her.

"You know, it's getting pretty late," Buffy said, clearly ready to change the subject, "and we still haven't talked about my English essay."

That was more like it. She obviously liked Todd. But she was nowhere near letting him get close to that inner sanctum she guarded so carefully. Trust was a huge issue with Buffy, and Angelus sensed that, despite the fact that Buffy seemed flattered by Todd's attentions, it was going to take more than a little flirting to break down the walls she had built around her heart.

Good girl, Angelus thought as he dropped silently from the roof onto Buffy's front yard and caught the faint scent of infant from a few houses down. He toyed with the idea of getting himself an invitation into that house, but sweet as newborn blood was, there wasn't usually enough there to do more than whet his appetite.

Maybe he should wait for Todd. Buffy had miles to go before she slept that night, and it sounded like their session was about to come to an end. The tutor would undoubtedly be heading out the front door in minutes. But then, how much more delicious would it be to wait for Buffy to actually develop a serious liking for Todd before Angelus sucked the life out of him? Today, Todd was a harmless flirtation. Given enough time, he could become someone Buffy would be truly sad to see die.

In his hundred-plus years of existence as a demon, Angelus had definitely learned patience. And when it came to Buffy, there was nothing worth having that wasn't worth waiting for.

Todd could wait.

For now.

Chapter Four

Buffy didn't want to think about Todd's dimples. She didn't want to think about how smart he was, or how normal he was, or what a nice change of pace it would be to spend time with a boy who didn't even know vampires were real, let alone how plentiful they were in this neck of the woods. She also didn't want to think about how much better she seemed to feel when Todd was around. Buffy's self-esteem had been one of Angel's many casualties of late, and it did her more good than she realized to feel another boy's attraction; especially such a cute boy's.

Mostly she didn't want to think about a civil war that had erupted in England almost a thousand years ago.

Her head was so full of all the things she didn't want to think about that as she sat poised over her world history textbook, highlighter in hand, she found all of those things coalescing into a vaguely blurry ball that buzzed and hummed until she was faintly aware that her eyes no longer wanted to stay open.

Patrol.

When that word came darting through the haze, Buffy found herself fully awake.

She also found that she was really, really cold.

Her room was exactly what it should be. The desk lamp glowed brightly, and the sky outside her open window, *hence the cold,* was still pretty dark.

What was I supposed to be doing? she found herself wondering.

Her textbook lay open before her, but a quick glance at the clock by her bed told her that almost the full night had somehow elapsed since she had asked Todd to leave so she could finish her assignments on her own. Of course this had been a flimsy excuse to get him out the door so she could do a little patrolling before going to bed.

Crap.

Now fully awake, and still too cold, Buffy rose and started to shut her bedroom window before accepting the fact that she would never hear the end of it from Giles for two nights in a row of zero slaying and that the window was as good a way as any to leave the house in the wee hours of the morning.

Grabbing her heavy leather jacket and a few spare stakes from the trunk in her closet, Buffy did a quick hallway check to confirm that Joyce was snoring softly in the next bedroom before she shimmied out her window and landed with a soft thud on her front lawn.

She honestly didn't know what was wrong with her. Though her sense of time was not as finely honed as your average vampire's, Buffy had often found that her internal clock was subconsciously sensitive to the passage of time. Many a night, walking these same streets with Angel, she had found herself growing anxious as part of her felt the approach of dawn, knowing this would require them to separate.

Stop thinking about Angel and concentrate, Buffy demanded of herself.

Despite the fact that her body had apparently forced a full night of sleep upon her, and the reality that she had lost valuable study and slaying time in the process, Buffy still had at least an hour before dawn and remained cautiously optimistic that something that shouldn't be was still probably lurking the streets of Sunnydale.

She decided to cut through the playground of a nearby park en route to the cemetery nearest the high school when she pulled herself up short before jumping a chain-link fence. In the faint moonlight she could barely make out the form of a young girl and she could hear the metallic whine of one of the playground's swings.

This couldn't be more wrong, Buffy thought immediately as a tiny bit of adrenaline pushed her into a hyper-conscious state. There was no rational explanation she could conceive of that would include a little girl on a swing set just before dawn. A memory forced itself into her consciousness: Giles . . . yesterday . . .

and something about a little girl who was missing. Buffy didn't like to let herself hope, but she quickened her steps as she approached the girl, and was gratified to see that as she did, the girl looked up and met Buffy's gaze shyly.

Immediately conscious that she should try to keep the little girl at ease, Buffy stopped a few paces short of the swing and knelt so as to address the girl at roughly eye level. "Hi, there," she said gently.

"Hi," the girl replied.

"My name's Buffy," the Slayer said. "What's yours?"

"Callie," the girl said with a faint smile as she pushed herself off from the ground a bit to start the swing going again.

Buffy cursed herself for not having paid more attention to Giles but thought that the name did sound vaguely familiar. Hopeful that she was on the right track, Buffy rose and took the swing next to Callie's before she continued.

"It's kind of late . . . or kind of early, to be playing, isn't it?" Buffy asked. "Do your parents know you're here?"

The girl shrugged and continued to swing.

"You know, the swings were always my favorite too. But I hate to think that someone might be out there missing you right now. Why don't you let me walk you home?" Buffy suggested.

"I'm hungry," was Callie's defiant response.

"Okay," Buffy said, rising and extending her hand to Callie. "Come to think of it, I'm pretty hungry too.

Maybe we could find a little something on the way back to your house."

"Do you like to eat people?" Callie asked sweetly. "Because I don't."

The transformation was instantaneous. One moment, blond ringlets had framed chubby cheeks and a perky little heart-shaped mouth, and the next, the girl's forehead protruded and the blue of her eyes was lost to a feral yellowish glow as the child-vampire's fangs extended themselves from her gruesome mouth.

Buffy was poised for action, a stake in her hand, before her mind even registered what was happening. She put a couple of feet between them and waited for a lunge, but Callie remained seated on the swing looking up at Buffy, almost sadly.

Buffy knew what she had to do. This was the easy part of the job. Find demon. Kill demon. Unless the demon had a soul, or had once been her boyfriend, it was rarely more complicated than that.

But she couldn't. This was a child.

No it isn't, another voice within her reasoned.

Time and again she and Giles had discussed the reality that, once a human was turned into a vampire, the human was gone. The vampire that remained might remember the details and relationships of their previous lives, but the body was all demon. There was nothing to be saved, no hope for the victim. This child had already been killed by a vampire. The fact that something newborn and evil now wore her face meant nothing. Callie was already dead.

Callie seemed to sense Buffy's reluctance. For the

first time since they'd met, she smiled broadly.

"What's wrong, Buffy?" Callie asked.

"Nothing," Buffy replied less forcefully than she would have liked.

"Then come and get me," Callie shouted, and sprang up.

Buffy instinctively jumped back to avoid the attack. She actually hit the ground butt first before she realized that Callie was now running off in the opposite direction.

She considered giving chase. Vampires were faster than humans, but so was Buffy. Even now she might still catch her. But something kept her rooted to the ground.

Buffy had never before faced a vampire who was a child. Now there was something else in the world she didn't know if she had the strength to kill.

She needed to talk to Giles.

Though she didn't think Giles would be at the library for another few hours, she knew he'd forgive the wake-up call, under the circumstances. Retracing her steps back toward her home, Buffy was running so quickly, she narrowly avoided smashing full-force into a pedestrian she encountered just a few blocks from Ravello Drive.

Though it seemed a bit early for a jog, Buffy had almost put it from her mind as she offered a quick apology, until she realized that the "jogger" wasn't so much jogging away from her as lumbering casually along as if he didn't have a care in the world.

Then it hit her.

"Principal Snyder?" Buffy said in disbelief.

The balding pate and unfortunately large ears were unmistakable, as was the civil servant's budget suit. For reasons that defied understanding, Buffy's principal was roaming the streets of Sunnydale before dawn like a sleepwalker.

Uh-oh.

Maybe Callie wasn't the only new vampire in town. But though she wouldn't have hesitated to strike down a vampire Snyder—in fact, she would have taken great pleasure in it—she knew in her gut that Snyder was still very much alive.

And limping?

Snyder walked on, favoring his left foot, oblivious of Buffy. Honing in on the principal's feet, she realized with alarm that he was barefoot, and leaving a distinct trail behind him.

Buffy couldn't smell blood, but she certainly knew it when she saw it. Kneeling at the closest part of the trail, Buffy satisfied herself that Principal Snyder's left foot was bleeding—rather copiously, from the looks of things.

It was too much. Something was seriously wrong with this picture, but between Callie and the reality of a new school day dawning on the horizon, Buffy decided that rather than confront the principal here and now, she needed a shower, a change of clothes, and a telephone . . . probably not in that order.

Well done, Rupert, Giles thought as he rose from the insufferable wooden chair before his small office desk in the school library, cursing the stiffness in his back and wondering how he had managed to fall asleep there, rather than in his perfectly comfortable bed at home. Truth be told, he couldn't remember.

It wasn't that sleeping in the library was such a rare occurrence. During many of Buffy's more complicated trials of the last few years he had burned more than his fair share of the midnight oil in this very spot. He even kept a few clean dress shirts and a toothbrush at the library for such occasions. But as there was nothing particularly apocalyptic on his schedule for the week, he found it odd that he'd lost track of time over a well-worn edition of Tomberlin's *Demons of Eighteenth-Century Europe*, and had dropped off for more than eight hours while seated at his desk.

An urgent call from Buffy had awakened him here, just short of six a.m. As he debated between boiling a kettle or firing up the coffeemaker in the faculty lounge, he realized that from the tone of Buffy's voice he had only minutes before she would come bursting into the library, so he opted to settle for a quick round of morning ablutions in the nearest restroom, followed by a fresh shirt.

By the time he'd returned to the library, Buffy was already waiting for him, seriously studying a number of large reference books he'd left on the main table.

"Good morning, Buffy," he greeted her.

"There you are," she shot back. How she could be peeved this early in the morning escaped him, but he had no doubt she would illuminate her problem as best she could with little prodding on his part.

"The little girl, the one you mentioned yesterday," Buffy began.

"Callie McKay?" Giles offered.

"I thought so," Buffy said, shaking her head.

"What happened?" Giles asked. "Did you find her?"

"I think so. Do you still have the paper?"

Giles hurried to his office, retrieved Monday's paper from the trash can and had opened it to the article about Callie's disappearance before he realized Buffy was right on his heels. He handed her the article, but the serious disappointment on her face as she studied the picture told him all he needed to know about Callie's fate.

"I'm sorry, Buffy," he offered gently. "I suppose we should alert her parents as to her . . . whereabouts. Where exactly did you find her?"

"At the park, swinging," Buffy replied angrily.

Giles was suddenly confused. He'd assumed Buffy had intended to confirm the identity of a body she'd found, but if the child was still alive . . .

"She wasn't—?" he began.

"Oh, she's dead," Buffy replied quickly. "In fact, she's undead."

"But . . ." Giles truly didn't know where to begin. "Are you certain?" he asked.

"She transformed right in front of me, Giles," Buffy countered. "How much more certain do I need to be?"

"It's just—"

"What?" Buffy demanded.

"W-well . . ." he stammered, "it's just that most vampires instinctively shy away from siring children as young as Callie."

"Then somebody's tossed out the rule book," Buffy replied, then added, "No prizes guessing who."

With all the questions running through Giles's head at the moment, it took him a few seconds to catch her meaning. "Angel?" he said.

"Sure." She shrugged. "You said he's big with the psychological warfare. I have to hand it to him. He did catch me off my guard this time."

For the first time since she'd called, Giles regretted not making some coffee. He didn't feel particularly well rested from his night sleeping upright, and it was already promising to be a spectacularly long day.

"Then I take it you found it difficult to—"

"Stake her?" Buffy finished for him.

"Yes."

"I didn't."

"What?" Giles said with genuine concern. "Didn't stake her, or didn't find it difficult?" he clarified, wondering who was responsible for teaching America's youth proper grammar, and wishing them all great bodily harm.

"She ran off before I had a chance."

Giles considered Buffy carefully. He had a hard time believing that Buffy couldn't have fairly easily dealt with one vampire, particularly an immature vampire.

Buffy looked into Giles's eyes, the battle between anger and sadness clearly raging. He instantly pitied her the encounter and the difficulty of the choice she'd faced that night. He had to remind himself again that much as she'd grown since he'd become her Watcher, she was still, in so many ways, just a girl.

"Buffy, you must understand that Callie is already dead. Her appearance may be startling, but she is still a demon and, unfortunately, must be destroyed," Giles said as compassionately as possible.

"I know," Buffy answered glumly. "But it was so strange."

"I can well imagine," Giles replied.

"She said she didn't like to eat people," Buffy offered. "Is that even possible?"

Giles paused before answering. "To be honest, Buffy, there is very little known about child-vampires. As I said, most vampires are extremely reluctant to turn children. Though they do gain the expected strength and stamina of an adult vampire, children do not mature instantly when they are turned. Though they couldn't be called innocent," he continued, choosing his words carefully, "they do tend to retain the willfulness and impulsiveness of their former age. They are difficult to manage and, frankly, usually more trouble than they are worth—at least from the point of view of a potential sire."

"I hesitated, Giles," Buffy said simply. "I knew what I had to do, but I just couldn't bring myself to do it."

"It's perfectly understandable," Giles said, placing

a comforting hand on Buffy's shoulder. "You were taken by surprise. But I must tell you, I have a hard time believing that Angelus would trouble himself to do this, despite your quite natural misgivings. I understand that dealing with Angel is your primary focus of late. But any number of vampires could have been responsible for this. Frankly, it strikes me as the act of either a very young, or a very unstable, demon."

"Either way, I guess I know what I have to do," Buffy said softly.

She turned away and started toward the doors. Giles struggled to find words to either comfort or inspire her, but he hadn't settled on any when she turned and said, "By the way, have you noticed anything odd about Principal Snyder the past few days?"

Giles had often suffered serious mental whiplash at the myriad twists and turns of his Slayer's mind, but this caught him entirely unprepared. "I beg your pardon?"

"After I saw Callie, I almost ran into Snyder. He was out for an early morning walk. But it was like he didn't even see me. And his foot was bleeding."

Though Giles found this puzzling, his focus on Callie and her affect on Buffy made him quick to dismiss it.

"Well, I'll make it a point to speak to him later, if you like, but I'm certain it's nothing to worry yourself about."

"Right," Buffy said.

"Your priority must be to find Callie," he reiterated.

"Got it." She nodded, then added, "Thanks for coming in early. I'm sorry I woke you."

"Never a problem," Giles said cordially as she disappeared into the hallway. "Have a good morning," he offered much too late.

"Wait . . . he was doing what?" Xander asked, pausing before he bit into a fried fish stick.

"He was walking down the street, just before dawn, and leaving a trail of fresh blood behind him," Buffy replied as she toyed with her fruit salad.

"What kind of socks was he wearing?" Willow asked.

"Can we not start with the socks again?" Cordelia pleaded, stifling a yawn.

"Guys, you're missing the point," Buffy said briskly. The entire gang had gathered in the cafeteria for lunch, Xander and Cordelia, Willow and Oz, and Buffy and her salad. Normally the sight of her friends and their respective romantic interests didn't trouble Buffy, but lately she had started to feel too much like a third, or in this case, fifth, wheel. Xander's passion for Cordelia had been difficult to accept in its early days, but over time, Buffy had come to terms with it. Willow's newer romance with the sweet but taciturn Oz, who'd only recently discovered he was a werewolf, was truly a source of happiness for Buffy. Still, there was something in the new couple's cuteness and playfulness that brought Buffy's loneliness into sharper focus than she could ever say. Most days it simply brought vivid images of all she'd lost in Angel to the forefront of her mind. On afternoons like this one, when she was both troubled by her slaying duties and insufficiently rested, it almost made her crabby.

"Am I the only one here who thinks that's just too weird?" Buffy continued as diplomatically as she could.

"I'd give it an odd, but I'd like to withhold 'weird' until we get a judge's ruling on the socks," Oz said simply.

"No, I'm with Buffy on this one," Willow decided. "Only because Snyder didn't say anything mean to her."

"Thanks, Wil," Buffy replied.

"So you're thinking demon, Buffy?" Xander asked.

"I don't know," she retorted sharply. "Giles didn't seem to think it was that big a deal."

"Then what are you worried about? If Mr. I'm-All-Smart-and-British doesn't care, I say let it go," Cordelia offered, clearly exasperated that Xander was, once again, paying more attention to Buffy than to her. "So the little twerp exercises. So he does it first thing in the morning. If you ask me, it's the most normal thing Snyder's ever done."

"Were your ears in the upright and open position when I mentioned the blood?" Buffy snapped.

"Maybe he cut himself shaving," Willow offered.

"How many men do you know who shave their toes?" Buffy asked.

"Well . . . ," Oz began.

But before he could continue, the attention of everyone at the table was drawn to the cafeteria line, where Larry, a likable enough jock who had recently and inadvertently revealed to Xander that he was gay, and Jonathan, a sweet, rather quiet junior who always seemed to find himself in the line of fire, were screaming at each other at the top of their lungs.

"I called dibs on the red Jell-O, man!" Larry shouted, shoving Jonathan into a gaggle of freshman girls who were trying to pay for their lunch at the counter.

Jonathan recovered quickly and shouted back, "What are you, five? There are no dibs in the lunch line! It's first come, first served."

The next few moments were a blur. Larry grabbed Jonathan by his shirt, and a few of Larry's football buddies who were behind him in line piled on as Jonathan started swinging for dear life. Without thinking, Buffy jumped into the fray, dodging punches and, with no small effort on her part, succeeded in pulling the entire Sunnydale High School offensive line off of Jonathan, who ended up on his back and covered in red Jell-O.

When everyone had settled for a moment, Buffy grabbed Larry and demanded, "What's the problem?"

"I don't know," Larry replied lamely. "I just wanted my Jell-O."

Buffy's anger downshifted to concern. Larry wasn't the brightest bulb in the package, but he was also no longer the overcompensating school bully she'd first come to know. He seemed as confused as she was by his actions. He shook his head and looked about, almost as if he were just now realizing where he was and what he was doing.

"Step away from the lunch line," Buffy said both calmly and commandingly, handing Larry his very own bowl of Jell-O and turning him toward the cashier.

"Right. Sorry," Larry said, then added, "I guess I'm just really tired. I don't think I slept last night. Maybe it's low blood sugar."

Buffy turned her attention to Jonathan and, as she helped him to his feet, suddenly realized that everyone in the cafeteria was now looking at her. *One of these days I'm going to remember to think before I act,* she chided herself. She didn't necessarily mind being the center of attention, but this really wasn't the kind of attention she enjoyed. Still, she was gratified to see that Larry and his buddies were moving slowly away from the lunch line.

"Thanks, Buffy," Jonathan said quietly.

"What got into you?" she asked him. "In what bizarro universe was that a fight you were going to win?"

"It pissed me off," Jonathan replied. "This is supposed to be high school. No one has seriously called dibs on anything since the fifth grade."

"Okay, but next time, you might want to think before you take on the entire football team over the last of the red Jell-O," Buffy said. "There's something to be said for picking your battles, you know?"

"I know. I'm just so tired of those guys picking on me. Really tired."

As he spoke, Jonathan stifled a yawn, and Buffy saw his eyes start to glaze over with weariness. All the energy seemed to drain from his face as he turned to find a lunch table.

That's weird, Buffy thought. One minute, they're at each other's throats, and the next . . . well, it wasn't a chorus of "Kumbaya," but it was pretty darn close. Her musings were interrupted by Cordelia, who, along with the others, had gathered her things from the lunch table and was heading for the door.

"Gee, Buffy, if this whole Slayer thing doesn't work out, you clearly have a brilliant future as a hall monitor," Cordelia said, grabbing Xander by the sleeve and dragging him into the hall.

"Stuff it, Cordelia," Willow snapped.

Cordelia feigned deafness to Willow's jab, but Buffy turned to her friend, concerned.

"Are you okay, Wil?" she asked.

Willow thought about it for a second longer than it usually would have taken.

"Yeah, I don't know."

"I mean, I know you're still the acting president of the I-Hate-Cordelia club, but that was a little harsh, don't you think?"

"I can't help it," Willow said defensively. "She just makes me cranky."

It seemed clear to Buffy that everyone had taken their edgy pills this morning. To lighten the mood she waited for a "Later, guys" from Oz as he headed upstairs to his next class and, lowering her voice to a conspiratorial level, she asked Willow, "So, last night . . . any good Oz dreams?"

Willow blushed instantly, but then seriously considered the question. "No," she finally replied remorsefully. "I don't remember any of my dreams from last night."

"Well, fear not," Buffy said, placing a playful arm over Willow's shoulder, "there's always tonight."

As they made their way through the hall, Buffy was stopped in her tracks by the sight of Principal Snyder standing outside the chemistry lab holding a freshman boy, whose name Buffy couldn't recall, by the ear.

"Sleeping in class, young man? Maybe on somebody else's campus," he said in his typical I-have-all-the-power tone.

Willow, Xander, and Cordelia immediately dodged into the nearest classroom to avoid Snyder. But Buffy paused, toying with the right way to ask the principal what the hell he'd been doing that morning, when he caught sight of her and, still holding the boy's ear, remarked with a snide smile, "Ah, Miss Summers, how goes the tutoring?"

It might have been a record. In less than a second Buffy had gone from actually worrying a little about the man to wishing she could have just a few minutes alone with him in a dark alley to teach him the meaning of power.

"It's going great, Principal Snyder," she replied, raising her chin in a small act of defiance.

"I hope so, for your sake." He smiled. "As I understand it, the tutor the school board recommended for you is the most demanding in the business. Not that I think it will do much good," he added with a deep sigh of satisfaction.

"He's great," Buffy replied, as if she wouldn't have wanted it any other way. "Really very helpful."

"Aren't you late for class?" Snyder asked, oblivious to the fact that he was still holding the freshman's ear and said freshman was writhing in considerable agony beneath his fingers.

"Nope. I have study hall this period," Buffy replied with a smile. "I'm library bound to complete some of my extra assignments."

"Well, what are you waiting for?" Snyder sneered. "Go."

Buffy did as he suggested. Only when she reached the library did it occur to her that Snyder was wearing the same suit today she'd seen him in earlier that morning, a light blue polyester blend, but he'd matched it with a pair of white wingtips that, apart from being out of season, were totally wrong for daytime.

Maybe his foot is still hurting, Buffy mused. She knew it was wrong to enjoy that thought, but she just couldn't help herself.

Buffy was a Slayer. Not a saint.

Chapter Five

Angelus was having the most delectable vision. Buffy was bound and gagged at his feet. Her friends Xander, Willow, and Giles were already eviscerated, their respective guts pouring from their bellies and spilling out onto the blood-soaked ground. Todd was kneeling before him, a picture of smarmy tutorial terror pleading for his life, when Angelus was startled out of his reverie by the sound of breaking glass. It only took a second to discern the direction from whence it had come, Drusilla's sitting room.

He flirted with the idea of leaving Dru and Spike to whatever they were doing, settling himself down to continue revising Todd's last moments of life, when a second shattering of glass and muffled raised voices met his ears.

What the hell?

He hurried down the main hall toward the master suite. Before he could enter, Callie flew past him screeching, pausing only to kick him hard in the shin before darting into the living room and jumping onto the couch, holding one of Dru's many precious china dolls above her head and shrieking, "You are not the boss of me!" at the top of her little lungs.

Dru was right behind her, alight with rage.

"Put her down, Callie," Dru demanded. "She sings beautiful songs to Mommy. Bring her to me at once!"

But that was all Callie needed to hear. The moment Dru made it clear that the doll meant something to her, Callie brought her arms down, thrusting the porcelain doll to the floor, where its face shattered when it met the hard stone.

"No!" Dru cried out, as if physically struck by the loss. She rushed to the floor and began gently picking up the pieces in a vain attempt to reassemble them.

"Welcome to the village of the damned," Spike offered drolly as he rolled himself into the entryway, holding Dru's beloved pet dog, Sunshine, on his lap.

Callie continued to rampage through the room, tearing into pillows, knocking over tables, and upending anything that wasn't nailed down.

"Oh, I don't think so," Angelus retorted sharply. In a few quick steps he was across the room, and grabbing Callie securely by the shoulders, bent to say firmly, "Callie, it's not nice to destroy Mommy's things. Now play nice and say you're sorry."

"Make me!" Callie screamed back, struggling in

Angelus's grasp and punctuating her disdain by attempting to bite his hand.

"Gladly," Angelus replied. His patience didn't extend to spoiled brats, and in a flash he had dragged Callie to the heavily curtained French doors that separated the living room from the main courtyard and opened them just enough to show Callie the bright patch of afternoon sun that still fell onto a corner of the patio.

"Sounds like someone needs a time-out," Angelus said as he threw open the doors with one hand and, with the other, tossed Callie unceremoniously toward the sunlight. As she struggled to regain her feet, Angelus noticed approvingly that one of her hands had tumbled into the light. It singed only slightly in a sweetly scented, smoky vapor before she pulled it back and retreated into the late afternoon shadows, hissing at him between cries of "Owie!"

Content for the moment, Angelus turned on Drusilla. "Look, honey, I know how much you love your pets," he began.

"Oh, Angelus, you musn't kill her," Dru pleaded.

"There's still plenty of shade out there for now. How else do you expect her to learn her lessons?" Angelus asked.

Dru nodded, turned mournfully to Spike, and began to sob. Angelus looked to Spike, who dumped Dru's little dog onto the floor, only increasing the intensity of her sobs.

"It seems Callie was a bit peckish and decided to have Mr. Sunshine here as her afternoon snack," Spike explained with just a hint of malicious glee.

"She stayed out all night, Angelus," Dru cried despondently, "but didn't eat a thing. I don't know what to do with her," she finally said mournfully. "She doesn't seem to love me at all."

"I told you when you brought her into this house that Callie was your responsibility, Dru," Angelus said menacingly. "I know you wanted a playmate, but if you can't control her . . ."

"Were you born at night or last night?" Spike shot back. "You don't control a child, particularly a child vampire. You stay the hell out of their way."

"I just wanted . . ." But Dru was again overcome by her anguish.

Angelus knelt beside Dru, placing a comforting arm around her shoulder. "There, there," he said gently. "She'll come around."

But instead of accepting Angelus's kindness, Dru rose quickly to her feet and said, "I can't do this alone. Callie needs her mommy and her daddies. She doesn't know how to hunt properly."

"Hunting isn't something you learn. It's instinct," Angelus retorted.

"She needs time," Dru countered.

"That may be, love," Spike interjected, "but I don't think the furniture can take it."

"Then what do you suggest?" Dru asked sharply, glaring at both Angelus and Spike in turn. "She's starving. She has to eat. You should go and find her someone so she's not tempted to snack between meals."

"I don't have time for this," Angelus replied.

"Right, you're too busy not killing the Slayer," Spike said.

Angelus answered him with a simmering glare before adding, "If she won't hunt for herself, send Mr. Meals-on-Wheels for take-out. I have better things to do." And with that, he stormed from the room.

Once he was out of earshot, Spike turned to Dru and said softly, "Why don't you let me have a go, pet?" Dru nodded forlornly, and Spike wheeled himself over to the doors and let himself onto the patio where Callie knelt in a shaded corner. Keeping well out of the light, Spike made his way to her, stopping a few feet short, but giving her no room to run far.

"I see we have a problem playing well with others," he said simply. "Lucky for you, I can relate."

Callie looked up at him, her fight clearly spent for the moment.

"A little birdie told me you don't think you want to eat people," he said gently. "Do you like people?" he asked. "Are you afraid to hurt them? Is that the problem?"

Callie shrugged. "It's just . . . wrong," she said finally.

"Wrong?" Spike asked.

"Like telling a lie, or cheating on a test in school," Callie clarified.

"I see." Spike nodded. "And you know, I agree. Standards, codes of conduct, aren't necessarily bad things. It's true, most vampires don't care who they eat, but if it's something you feel strongly about, I think we can work with it." He paused, watching her closely and pleased to see that she was hanging on his every word. "Let me ask you this, pet. Are all people good? Does everyone care as much as you do about telling the truth or earning their grades?"

Callie seemed to seriously consider the question.

Spike continued to lead her on. "I mean, aren't there people you know who used to be mean to you, or upset you?"

Callie's bright eyes met Spike's. "Michael," she said softly.

"Michael?" Spike asked. "And what did Michael do to you?"

"He teased me on the playground," Callie said. "He never let me on the swings."

"Sounds to me like Michael needs to learn a lesson or two, doesn't it," Spike said gently.

For the first time since they'd met, Callie actually smiled at Spike, and for reasons that he couldn't place, it felt almost . . . good.

"I could definitely eat Michael," she said, "But how do I find him? At night, he'll be at home, and I don't know where he lives."

"You let me worry about that, little one," Spike said, reaching out a hand to help Callie up. After a moment, she took it and clambered up onto his lap.

"Is there anyone else you can think of?" Spike asked.

"Tony!" Callie smiled, clapping her little hands.

Spike wheeled the two of them back into the living room as Callie whispered to him her stories of Tony, and Adam, and a number of other boys and girls who in very short order were going to seriously regret not having been nicer to Callie when she was alive.

Dru stood near the fireplace, watching them anxiously as they entered. With a slight wink to Dru, which was rewarded by one of her most vicious smiles, Spike encouraged Callie to tell him more about the children she disliked. Twenty minutes later, a much happier Callie had fallen into a deep slumber, curled up on his lap.

"My Spikey has a way with children," Dru cooed lovingly.

Spike accepted the compliment, along with the subtle satisfaction of having succeeded in doing that which pleased Dru and alienated Angelus. If he could drive Callie between them, it would be well worth the effort. Besides, against all laws of nature, he found he was truly beginning to like the child. Maybe it was the fierceness of her passions. Or maybe it was the way she had looked at him earlier when she'd first glimpsed the ease with which pain could be transformed into evil. Either way, this was turning out to be a much better day than he'd reckoned when he'd first found Callie feeding on Sunshine not an hour earlier. After so many months of neglect and frustration, Spike had found someone who might come to love him almost as much as Drusilla did, but who, more than that, could offer him something Drusilla hadn't in months.

Callie might just *need* him.

Buffy's day had taken a definite upturn following lunch. She'd actually joined in on a class discussion on Keats, receiving a series of surprised compliments from her English teacher, Mrs. Massey, and felt she'd done extremely well on a world history pop quiz. Though she wasn't going to be winning an academic decathlon anytime soon, Buffy had to admit that the extra study time with Todd was already paying off. By the time she got home, she was actually looking forward to seeing him, and found that he was already waiting for her in her bedroom.

To her surprise, Todd seemed startled by her. He rose abruptly from the seat by her dresser, quickly slamming shut one of the drawers and smiling as if he was trying to hide something. "Oh, hi, Buffy," he said quickly.

"You're early," she replied warily. A small knot formed in her stomach as she realized that the drawer he had just been snooping in was one of her emergency drawers, containing a few crucifixes and some holy water. Not hard to explain if you were contemplating entering a convent, but a little out of the ordinary for your average high school junior.

Buffy considered trying to come up with an excuse for the drawer's contents, but opted against it. He had no business going through her personal things, and if it weren't for her mother, the school board, and the fact that she was actually learning something, she might have physically thrown him from her house right then and there.

Todd seemed to sense the tension in her silence and said, "I don't know about you, but I'm pretty thirsty. How about I get us a couple of sodas before we start?"

"Sure," Buffy answered, still on guard.

A few minutes later he was back, two tall glasses in hand, and Buffy did her best to shake the ick factor. It was probably nothing. Just curiosity. And if Todd wanted to know more about her, maybe that was a good thing. At least it hadn't been her underwear drawer.

Still, as they tackled her chemistry chapters, her mind refused to stay on topic.

"It's official," she declared a few hours later. "Organic molecules suck."

"Oh, go easy on the poor molecules," Todd teased. "They don't mean to be so complicated."

"There is no way any future version of me is going to use chemistry," Buffy replied, refusing to give in to Todd's charms.

"You don't know that," he replied.

"Oh, but I do."

"Things change all the time, Buffy. None of us can see the future. You know how it is. One minute you think you have it all figured out, and the next, out of the blue, something totally unexpected happens."

Todd's eyes caught Buffy's. There was something almost hopeful in them. But it was quickly clouded over by doubt.

"I mean, who knows?" Todd continued. "Give chemistry a chance and you might just see more than math and particles. There's mystery in chemistry too."

"I usually like a good mystery," Buffy found herself saying before she could help herself.

Todd smiled.

Buffy returned the smile, and for a moment, that tiny withering garden in Buffy's secret heart saw a few fresh sprigs of green pushing themselves up through the earth. She found herself turning away, trying to push the hope that had started to rise back into its box before someone got hurt.

Because, in her experience, someone always got hurt—and it was usually Buffy.

Her gaze fell on her open bedroom window. Across the street, her neighbor Mr. Hall was watering his front yard.

"It's getting a little chilly, isn't it?" Todd said, more to break the silence than anything.

"Oh, my bad," Buffy replied quickly. Crossing to the window she placed her hands firmly on the frame to shut it when the sight of Principal Snyder walking casually past Mr. Hall caught her attention. He walked in the same measured gait that was both odd and troubling, and he was still wearing his white wingtips.

Her Slayer senses tingling, Buffy searched for a reasonable excuse to end her tutoring session a little early. She was surprised to find that, for once, the truth would make a compelling case.

"You know," she said, smiling apologetically, "I think organic molecules have turned my brain to mush. On top of that, I feel like I didn't sleep at all last night. Would you mind if we waited until Saturday to get back to history?"

Todd nodded, his disappointment obvious, but he covered nicely, saying, "No problem. I'm actually a little tired myself. We'll do the quizzes on chapters twenty through twenty-two first thing Saturday afternoon, deal?"

"Absolutely," Buffy agreed.

Buffy watched Todd make his way down her front walkway and was pleased to see that his road home led in the opposite direction from Snyder. As her mother would be working late tonight on inventory, Buffy quickly scrawled a note to her indicating that she was headed for the library, before exiting through the back door and cutting through a few neighbors' yards to catch up with the principal, not far from where she'd found him that morning.

Her hunch had been accurate. She found the principal crossing the first main intersection east of Ravello Drive, and with practiced ease had no difficulty keeping him in sight for the next six blocks as he walked slowly toward the southeast section of Sunnydale. Doing some quick mental geography, Buffy decided he was heading for Arborville, a development built in the early 1940s that had been a lovely neighborhood in its day. Unfortunately its day had come and gone, and now most of the houses in that area withered under the neglect of the retirees who no longer had the resources or the inclination to keep them properly maintained.

Snyder walked slowly, as if he was out for an afternoon stroll through the park. When he came to a four-way intersection at Oak Street, he turned south. Unfortunately, a driver turning left into Snyder's path probably didn't even see him in the early evening gloom.

Within seconds, Buffy threw herself into the car's path, knocking Snyder out of the way as the car screeched, then swerved to avoid the pedestrians, and ended up plowing into one of dozens of stately oak trees that lined the thoroughfare, giving it its name.

Buffy's first thought was for the principal. He picked himself up off the ground, without bothering to wipe the gravel from his hands or knees, and continued on his walk as if nothing had happened.

Definitely a ten on the weird-o-meter, Buffy decided. But before she could continue after him, she realized that the horn of the car that had hit the tree was blaring incessantly and traffic had slowed as other commuters tried to make their way around the accident.

Buffy's concern momentarily got the better of her curiosity. She approached the car and saw that the driver was crumpled over the steering wheel, his head resting on the horn. Buffy quickly opened the driver's door and asked, "Hey, are you all right?"

The driver didn't respond. Given that the car's collision with the tree had been fairly low impact, and there was no blood or even a scratch on the driver's face, Buffy wondered how the driver could have been knocked unconscious by the accident. She gently lifted the driver's head from the horn and set him upright in his seat. To her amazement, she heard a series of soft snores. The man wasn't injured. He had simply fallen asleep at the wheel.

"Hey, miss!" A voice interrupted Buffy's thoughts. Turning, she saw that another driver had pulled to the side of the road. "Everything okay?"

"Can you call 911?" Buffy asked, *or maybe the sandman,* Buffy thought to herself, and with a nod, the Good Samaritan was on his cell phone, alerting the police.

"An ambulance is on its way," the driver called back. In the confusion, it finally dawned on Buffy that she had lost sight of the principal. Hurrying back to the last corner where she'd seen him, she searched the increasing darkness for any sign of him but was quickly disappointed.

He probably couldn't have gone far. Once she heard the sounds of the approaching ambulance, satisfied that the driver was in good hands, Buffy took off down the street. Within a few minutes she had doubled back to the nearest main intersection and followed the opposite direction, until she was nearing Sunnydale's quaint main street, a series of storefronts and coffee shops flanked on one end by the old movie theater.

Her gut told her that now, she would probably never find the principal, and she had almost decided to simply cut her losses and sweep back through a few parks in search of Callie when she saw a familiar figure talking animatedly into a pay phone that bordered the town's central square.

It was Todd. Though his voice was low, his body language told her loudly and clearly that he was arguing with someone on the other end of the line.

Buffy considered just approaching him, but almost

as quickly decided that she didn't have a good excuse to be out walking the streets at night when she had ended their session so early. She closed the distance between them, finally pausing behind a nearby tree. Her stealth was rewarded, though her conscience pained her a bit. Just a few hours ago she had been frustrated with Todd for snooping around in her things, and here she was actually spying on him.

"No!" Todd said vehemently into the phone. After a pause: "I know what we agreed, but I'm saying I can't do it. I won't do it!" he finished forcefully.

Buffy had to admit, it was intriguing; maybe not crosses and holy water intriguing, but definitely, oddly interesting. This was not the gentle, sweet, and concerned boy she'd spent so much time with over the last few days. This Todd struggled to keep his voice down, clearly conscious that he was in a public place from the furtive glances he threw all around him as he talked. Furthermore, he was obviously angry. He seemed almost like a cornered animal, lashing out. A quick pang in her stomach told Buffy that suddenly Todd was more than a cute boy—now he was a cute boy with a secret, and though most of the secrets Buffy had unearthed in recent months hadn't been cuddly kittens, they *had* been worth knowing.

"There's more to him than meets the eye, wouldn't you say, sweetheart?" a familiar voice said behind Buffy.

Instantly her hand was searching her coat pockets for a stake, and the blood pumping through her veins had turned to ice.

"I'm sure I don't know what you're talking about," Buffy said stiffly as she turned to face Angelus.

He stood a few yards away, his arms crossed as he leaned against another tree, his expression one of smug pleasure that Buffy had only recently come to know and hate.

Her senses divided between keeping an eye on Angelus and protecting the unaware Todd, Buffy forced herself to keep one ear on the conversation going on behind her as she stepped gingerly toward Angelus's striking range and was rewarded seconds later by the sound of "Just tell him what I said," followed by the receiver slamming into the phone hook and Todd's steps hurrying obliviously up the street.

"Sure you do, Buffy," Angelus answered. "I get the distinct impression that *Todd* "—he drew out the vowel sound in a jeer that made Buffy want to pummel him—"has the hots for his new student."

"How do you—" Buffy started to ask, but stopped herself quickly, unwilling to allow him to see any surprise that he was keeping on top of every new development in her life. Of course he knew who Todd was. That was his style, even before he'd turned evil. Instead, she forced herself to smile, as if she were delighted by Todd's potential attraction, and replied, "Well, he wouldn't be the first, would he?"

Angelus's pose lost some of its nonchalance. Buffy wouldn't permit herself to imagine that Angelus was threatened by her interest in Todd. That would have been flattering. But sick and twisted as it was, that's exactly what seemed to emanate from Angelus as he stepped toward her.

"Careful, Buffy," Angelus warned.

"Oh, now I'm scared," Buffy taunted right back. "If I remember right, you used to kill first, ask questions . . . never. You want me dead. What's the holdup?"

"Sometimes I like to play with my food," Angelus replied charmlessly.

They were now both poised for battle. Ten kinds of tension cracked between them like a whip.

"Jealous much?" Buffy asked sweetly.

Angelus threw back his head and laughed, but there was no joy in it.

"Get over yourself," he replied.

"You first," she tempted, then dropped her right shoulder as if she was about to turn away and, as he instinctively moved in, rewarded him with a quick spin-kick that landed squarely mid-shoulder and sent him reeling to his left.

Once the battle was on, all thoughts melted away. There was nothing in the world but this moment, this fight. There were plenty of demons that Buffy could fight these days with half a night's sleep and one hand tied behind her back. Angelus wasn't one of them.

The past few times they'd met like this, Buffy had developed the distinct impression that Angelus was toying with her. He parried her punches and kicks with a graceful ease, never inflicting too much damage when he went on the assault. She pressed hard, taking each advantage that came her way; forcing Angelus farther from the main street, leading him into the more densely wooded park.

Once they'd found a little privacy, Buffy intensified her attack. A solid punch to his head sent him reeling back, and she followed it with a roundhouse kick that knocked him to the ground. In any other fight, this would have been the moment to go for the kill, but Buffy stepped back, not from fear or hesitation but simply because she knew Angelus and how he fought. He was trying to lure her into a position that would reverse their momentum. He wasn't seriously damaged by anything she had inflicted so far, and he wasn't tired. But if she hadn't fought by his side a hundred times before this, she would never have suspected it.

He rose from the ground with a smile on his face. "That all you got, gorgeous?"

"Oh, I'm just getting warmed up," she replied, catching her breath.

Angelus's retort was a direct charge that threw Buffy to the ground on her back. He tried to pin her down, but she carried his weight forward, throwing him off, and scurried in the opposite direction as he recovered.

"Looks like someone's learning some new moves," Angelus taunted. "Is your little hot Toddy teaching you more than history? Almost makes me sorry I was your first. I might have actually enjoyed myself if you'd known a little something about men instead of making me do all the work."

There were two interesting pieces of information in this last remark for Buffy. The first was that Angelus knew at least some of the specifics of her study sessions with Todd, which would indicate that he was watching her more closely than she was aware. The second was that even though he was hiding it in an insult, he really didn't like the idea of anyone being closer to her than he was.

Of course those two thoughts would only rise to Buffy's conscious mind several hours later when she was replaying the fight in her head and dissecting it, free from the emotional intensity of the immediate conflict. All she heard at that moment were the words "sorry I was your first."

She'd told herself a thousand times that the things Angelus said to hurt her had nothing to do with what Angel might really have thought about their first and last night together. But every time Angelus pricked her with this particular barb, Buffy immediately wanted to claw at his eyes, pound his face into a bloody pulp, and refuse to let up until he was a mangled, miserable, tortured shadow of his former self.

But even this short time to grieve had taught her something else. Angelus wasn't the only one who knew how to play dirty in a fight.

So instead of lashing out with her fists, she rose calmly from her crouch and, squaring her shoulders, said simply, "What Todd and I do in my bedroom is none of your concern. He's taught me things that a cold, lifeless stiff like you never could. He's not one to waste his time whoring and gambling and drinking himself into oblivion like you did back in the day; he's worked hard to earn what's his. He pleases me, Angel, on a level you never could."

For a moment, there was silence. Angelus seemed to pale a little more in the moonlight, but that could have been a trick of the darkness. Only when he leaped forward, throwing her to the ground and pinning her hands above her head, did Buffy feel a tiny surge of delight in knowing that she had actually managed to hurt him.

He lowered his face to hers, giving her a moment to fear the fury she saw in his eyes even as the Slayer inside her sought a maneuver that would throw him off of her.

"Never forget this," Angelus hissed. "There is nothing you can love in this world that I cannot take away from you."

"No, Angel," she replied, "there is nothing in this world that you can keep me from loving—not anymore."

Angelus's grip around her wrists tightened. But she no longer worried about having pushed him too far. Finally, he was the one who was knocked off balance by her. The power of this knowledge was intoxicating.

She was about to embrace the advantage and throw him off her, setting her up for the kill, when he bent his face closer, his lips almost touching hers.

"Finally," he said softly.

Finally what? A part of her mind that she refused to give voice to demanded.

But he answered her unspoken question when he continued, "You're almost worth killing."

"And you're almost a bad memory," she replied, thrusting her knee into his back.

But her knee met empty air. In a flash, Angelus was gone and Buffy rolled over onto the ground, winded and weak. She waited for the sobs to come, rising from the depths of her wounded heart and pouring out onto the dry earth.

They didn't.

Instead, a cold chill made her shudder as she realized that, great as her victory this night was, it had come at a price that would probably cost Todd his life.

Chapter Six

There was no easy way for Buffy to tell Todd everything he needed to know about the danger in which she had unintentionally placed him. She knew that somewhere out there a Slayer handbook existed. Kendra had told her about it shortly after they'd met and Giles had confirmed its existence though admitted he'd never shown it to her because he hadn't felt it would do much good. As she toyed with the telephone in her bedroom, Buffy wondered if "Uncomfortable Conversations with Cute Boys Who Might Want to Date You" was a chapter she'd find there.

If she ever learned that it was, she was going to kill Giles for not sharing, but she seriously doubted the words "Cute Boys" even appeared in the handbook, unless they were followed by the words "are usually eaten alive by . . ."

She did the best she could. At least Todd hadn't answered the phone when she called, so she managed an almost intelligible message, including the high points of the jealous ex-boyfriend who had learned that Todd was tutoring Buffy, and not inviting any strangers into his home if he could help it. Truth was, if Angel wanted Todd dead, there was little short of guarding him twenty-four hours a day she could do to protect him, and somehow she knew Giles would never go for that idea. At any rate, she was pretty sure that Todd wasn't going to be looking at her with that sweet, mysterious kind of hope in his eyes anymore once he heard her message. Maybe it was for the best. Besides, what was with that angry phone call near the park?

Then again, who died and made me center of the universe? Buffy thought as she changed into her pajamas. Odds were, whatever Todd was so upset about had nothing at all to do with her.

Contrary to her usual routine, Buffy's head hit the pillow within minutes of hanging up the phone. It was as if her pre-bedtime ritual of an hour of anxious love-life ruminations had never existed. The next thing Buffy was conscious of, the sun was sweeping through her bedroom window and her alarm was blaring in her ear. Unfortunately she still felt as though she'd been up all night.

As she entered the kitchen, she realized with alarm that she wasn't the only one in her house this morning who was sleep-challenged. Joyce stood before the stovetop, a griddle of burning pancakes before her. Even the rancid smoke rising to her nose wasn't enough to wake her. Buffy's mom was literally asleep on her feet.

"Mom!" Buffy shouted, startling Joyce into a conscious state as she grabbed the griddle and moved it off the stove and into the sink.

"Where am I?" Joyce muttered.

"Trying to set the kitchen on fire," Buffy said, running water over the griddle and forcing the burnt pancakes down the garbage disposal. "And while I appreciate the effort, haven't we discussed avoiding heavy machinery until you've had your coffee?"

"I'm sorry, honey," Joyce replied, moving gingerly toward the coffeepot and pouring herself a large cup. "I don't think I slept a wink last night."

"Are you still doing inventory?" Buffy asked.

"Am I? No, we finished yesterday afternoon," Joyce replied. "I guess I'm overtired."

"Stress will do that to you," Buffy said, then added, "Maybe you should take the day off and get some rest."

"Don't be ridiculous," Joyce snapped. "Haven't you come across the definition of the word 'responsibility' in any of your tutoring sessions?"

"Easy, Mom. It was just a suggestion," Buffy replied, a little wounded by Joyce's tone.

"I know, Buffy. I'm sorry," Joyce said sincerely. "I don't know what's wrong with me this morning."

"Hopefully nothing that a bowl of cornflakes won't cure," Buffy replied, pouring cereal for them.

"I think your faith in the power of corn might be misplaced, but I guess it's worth a try." Joyce smiled. "At least they don't have to be cooked."

Fifteen minutes later, Buffy was on her way out the door to join her mother in the car when the phone rang. "Hello?" she answered briskly.

"Hey, Buffy, it's Todd," came a slightly husky morning voice through the receiver.

Damn.

"Hi, Todd," Buffy said, attempting to sound as cheerful as possible. It wasn't that she didn't want to hear from him. She just wasn't looking forward to hearing him tell her that he didn't tutor crazy people and ending their relationship right then and there.

"I got your message," he began.

Here we go.

"Okay," she replied.

"It was . . ."

Insane?

"Really sweet of you to worry about me," he finished.

Buffy heaved an audible sigh of relief.

"It's probably nothing," she lied, "I just . . . I've had problems in the past—"

"Oh, you don't have to explain," he interjected. "I was just wondering . . ."

"Yes?"

"Well, we're only supposed to do four sessions a week, but I thought you might want to get together tonight."

"Oh." Buffy smiled in genuine surprise.

"Or, if you're not up for it, maybe we could just get some coffee, or something. . . ."

Joyce lay on the horn from the driveway, and

Buffy jumped.

"I'd really like that," Buffy said honestly. "Thing is, I'm not sure what the rest of my day is going to be like yet. Can I call you later?"

"Sure," he replied, Buffy's spirits rising even more at the faint disappointment she was sure she heard in his voice.

"Great," she said. "Talk to you soon."

"Can't wait."

Willow didn't know what was wrong with her. Ms. Hegel was giving a perfectly fascinating lecture on the symbolism of dreams, and she'd been keeping her dream journal for weeks in preparation for this section of her life sciences course, excluding, of course, her favorite recurring dream that featured her and Oz swimming in the inflatable backyard pool Xander had popped when he and Willow were seven. Sometimes she was naked in the dream, though Oz was always fully clothed, and usually wearing mittens. Still, she didn't think that particular dream was any of Ms. Hegel's business, so she hadn't felt too bad about leaving it out. The only other omission in the journal was for the past few days and that hadn't been intentional. Willow simply didn't remember having any dreams since Monday, and she didn't think she'd be graded down for that since she already had two full spiral notebooks completed on the assignment.

The problem was, she couldn't concentrate. Though Ms. Hegel seemed less perky than usual, Willow didn't think that was the issue. Xander sat next to her, his head resting in his right hand, eyes closed, and a small pool of drool collecting on his desktop. Behind him, Cordelia's head kept nodding forward only to snap back up every thirty seconds or so.

Two rows back, it sounded like Susan Walker and Ellie Thompson were training for a synchronized-snoring competition. In fact, everyone in class was either asleep or on the verge, and Willow herself felt like she could easily have nodded off without any effort at all. Ms. Hegel droned on, seemingly oblivious, which was also most unusual.

No matter what she did, Willow couldn't force herself to concentrate. Stifling a yawn, she opened her textbook to the section Ms. Hegel was covering, determined to read along, when she paused over the section immediately preceding that on dream symbolism, entitled "Sleep Disorders."

Five minutes later, Willow had excused herself from class and was headed for the library. She had been tempted to wake Xander, but he looked so cute when he was asleep. And he would have insisted on bringing Cordelia, which was never a plus, as far as Willow was concerned.

When she arrived, she was pleased to see that Buffy was already there, talking with Giles.

"No, Giles," Buffy was saying. "A ballpoint pen. Jeff was convinced Steven stole it and two seconds later, they were at each other's throats. Just like Larry and the Jell-O yesterday. I'm telling you, all is not as quiet on the Hellmouth as you promised a few days ago. Either everyone here ate some serious cranky puffs for breakfast, or something more demon-y than usual is getting on everyone's last nerve."

"As I said, Buffy," Giles said wearily, "the end of the year is a very stressful period for the students and the faculty. No one gets much sleep until finals are over—"

"Try *any* sleep," Willow interrupted.

"I beg your pardon," Giles said.

"Hey, Wil," Buffy added. "What do you mean, 'any sleep'?"

"We're studying dreams in my science class today. Well, me and Ms. Hegel are. Everyone else is in dreamland . . . or lack of dreamland."

"In something resembling English, please, Willow," Giles said.

Willow opened her textbook to the "Sleep Disorders" section as patiently as she could. She noted that Giles's eyes were bloodshot as he took a moment to clean his glasses and look over the text.

"There are five stages of sleep," Willow began. "Alpha state is the first and lightest."

"Willow, am I going to be tested on this material, or is there an abridged version of this theory somewhere?" Buffy interjected.

"Okay," Willow said, cutting to the chase, "the sleep stages where we actually get our rest occur around REM, the fifth and most important stage of sleep. It's called REM because there's rapid eye movement along with increased respiration and deep muscle paralysis at the same time. You move through all the stages of sleep several times a night, but if you never reach REM sleep, you're not really sleeping deeply enough."

"So you think no one is getting enough REM sleep?" Buffy said. "But how do you know?"

"What did you dream about last night, Buffy?"

Buffy paused. "Nothing. I mean, I don't remember."

"Giles?" Willow asked.

"Well . . . nor do I," he admitted.

"REM sleep is also when you dream. When you are deprived of REM sleep long enough, even after just a few days, there are serious side effects."

"Do they by any chance include sleepwalking?" Buffy asked, immediately beginning to connect the Principal Snyder dots.

"They do." Willow nodded. "The also include lapses in concentration, increased anxiety and irritability, and fatigue."

"Then it is your belief that the vast majority of the student body is having their sleep disturbed?" Giles asked.

"It makes sense," Buffy said. "I remember going to sleep every night this week, but I don't remember dreaming at all and, to be honest, I feel like I could nap for a week right now." Turning to Willow, she asked, "Is Snyder causing this? Because I wouldn't mind punishing him for a change."

Willow shook her head. "I don't think so. It seems more like he's a victim, like the rest of us."

"Well, can't have everything," Buffy said in obvious disappointment.

"We have to figure out what it is," Willow continued. "Giles, are there any references to demons that could cause this sort of thing?"

Giles shook his head. "Off the top of my head, I'd have to say no. What you're suggesting is very specific and sounds more like a spell than demonic intervention."

"Do you mind if I take a look?" Willow asked.

"Of course not." Giles nodded.

"I'll help," Buffy said. "Chemistry class was cancelled this afternoon. Mr. Olsen didn't show up *or* call in, so no one thought to get a substitute."

"Actually, Buffy, there's something else we need to discuss."

"What?" Buffy asked, alarmed.

In response, Giles placed the morning paper in front of her and opened it to an article about an attack on a second grade T-ball team that had taken place the night before. Buffy stared in shock at a picture of a mother holding the body of her son, eight-year-old Michael Holmes, and sobbing amidst the chaos of several ambulances and police cars in the parking lot of a local park.

"Are there Cliff's Notes?" Buffy asked, noting that the article covered the entire page and was continued in another section of the paper.

"Two young boys, Michael Holmes and Adam Neilson, were attacked last night after a practice session. The coach who was supposed to be looking after them until their parents arrived apparently left to help a disabled man who was having difficulty crossing the street. A parent leaving the parking lot described the man as having light blond hair and using a wheelchair. She also indicated that she thought he might have had a British accent."

"Spike," Buffy said grimly.

"I think it's also worth noting that both boys were classmates of Callie McKay's," Giles added somberly. "I take it you didn't come across either Spike or Callie while you were patrolling last night?"

"No," Buffy replied. "I had my hands full keeping Angel in check."

"I've got it!" Willow announced from the other side of the table. "A Siberian Sleeping Sloth."

"Only able to survive in the remotest regions of northern Russia," Giles answered briskly.

"I'm sorry, Giles," Buffy said sadly. "I'll find her tonight. I promise."

"If Spike has taken her under his wing, there's no telling—"

"I know," Buffy interrupted, "though he doesn't strike me as the father-knows-best type."

"I agree," Giles replied. "In your encounter with Angel, did you confront him about Callie?"

"No," Buffy confessed. "He's been spying on me, and my new tutor. I think Todd made Angel's most-wanted list last night. I honestly forgot all about Callie."

Giles shook his head in obvious disapproval.

"Really, really sorry," Buffy added. "I promise I'll find them tonight. Maybe I could get a jump on it this afternoon."

"Good." Giles nodded.

"What about a Somnambulatory Shudder-moth?" Willow piped up. "Or a Helvorkian Sleep Shaker?"

"The first is mythological, and the second has been extinct for five hundred years," Giles replied.

"In the meantime . . . ?" Buffy asked.

"I'll help Willow," Giles agreed.

The most difficult part of Buffy's assignment for the afternoon was zeroing in on a place to start looking. Since the factory where Spike, Drusilla, and Angel stayed had been destroyed in a fire, she had no idea where she might find the unholy trio and their new cabbage patch killer. She was loading up her backpack at her locker and contemplating playing "Kick the Crap out of the Demon" with Willy the Snitch for a lead when she caught sight of the principal leaving his office for the day. He passed her in the hall with a far-away smile on his face and not even a glance of insult in her direction. Buffy noted that he was no longer wearing the white wingtips with the blue suit. Instead, the principal was actually wearing a pair of faded red sneakers. Buffy did a little quick math in her head, try-ing to account for the array of natural disasters that would have to have occurred for Principal Snyder to be caught dead wearing those shoes in public, never mind leaving campus before the school day was over.

A whole lot of nothing came to mind, and as there was plenty of time until sundown, Buffy decided that she could easily keep her promise to Giles and still satisfy her raging curiosity about Snyder. The man had changed more than his footwear in the last few days, and Buffy wanted to know why.

Maybe Willow's wrong and this is *his fault,* she thought with an inward smile.

Buffy followed Snyder off campus and into the streets of Sunnydale at a safe distance and within twenty minutes was, once again, on the road to Arborville.

Snyder managed to avoid any close calls reminiscent of the night before as he trundled along, and a few times Buffy got close enough that she could have sworn she heard him humming softly under his breath while he walked. The sun was starting to fall toward the horizon, and Buffy was beginning to worry that she might have to let the principal go and start searching for Callie, when he turned down a street lined with houses buried deep within the old suburban district.

Come on, come on, Buffy pleaded silently. This was as off the beaten path as it was possible to get. She scanned the street as she walked. Many of the houses lining the street looked deserted, and those that weren't were still several gallons of paint shy of presentable. Apart from the loud barking of a really cranky-sounding dog and the rattling of a chain-link fence, she didn't sense any potential dangers unless you counted the serious lack of curb appeal.

Finally, Snyder reached a house at the end of the street and turned up the front walk.

Hallelujah, Buffy rejoiced inwardly. Only when she turned up the path herself did it dawn on her that she might have spent the last hour and a half accomplishing nothing but determining Snyder's home address. As she contemplated the overgrown front yard, the peeling paint, and the rotting boards overhanging the front porch, she was surprised to find herself thinking, *If this is all he has to come home to each night, no wonder he's such a miserable excuse for a human being.*

Snyder had reached the front door. Buffy ducked behind a dead jacaranda tree and waited for him to let himself in.

He did.

Just not the old-fashioned way.

Chapter Seven

Snyder didn't bother with the doorbell or knocker. In fact, he didn't bother with the doorknob. Instead, he stepped into what should have been a solid wood door and was quickly enveloped in a burst of blinding white light.

When Buffy's vision had cleared, the porch was empty.

I knew it! Buffy thought, thrilled to finally have some proof that her instincts about the principal had been right. She couldn't wait to tell Giles and Willow she told them so.

But at that point it dawned on her that now that she'd learned part of the truth, she was duty bound to figure out the rest. With a sigh, she hurried up to the porch and, pausing only for a second, walked into the front door. "Ow!" Buffy said aloud.

All she received for her trouble was a solid thwack on the head.

Stepping back, Buffy reached for the door. Running her hand over the worn surface, she decided it felt real enough.

But she knew what she'd seen. This was definitely not just a door. Normal doors didn't go all lite-brite when one person entered and then turn solid again. She considered knocking, or simply breaking it down, then thought better of it. With all that Snyder had against her, she didn't need to add stalking to the list, and stealth could be fun in small doses.

Searching the rest of the porch, she saw two windows on either side of the door. Both had been boarded up for years, if the cracked paint and rusty nails were any indication.

Buffy quickly pried one of the heavy planks from the window nearest the door and peered into the darkness. All she could make out was a faded, dusty, cobweb-covered sofa placed before a low table, also shrouded in webs. There was no sign that any human being, or Snyder, had inhabited the house in years.

A few more boards and a broken window later, Buffy climbed into the living room and allowed her eyes to adjust.

It was worse than staking out a cemetery. At least there you had the outdoors, the moonlight, and some really spectacular engraving work to look at. To see the faded, moth-eaten tablecloth and dusty plastic fruit arrangement centered perfectly on the dining table opposite the living room gave Buffy a whole new kind of creeps. Someone had lived here. Someone had made this a home. Someone had cross-stitched a "Home Sweet Home" pillow for the center of the sofa, and that someone had obviously died, leaving no one to care for their earthly possessions. It was sad.

It was also empty.

Buffy cautiously made her way through each room of the main floor, disturbing nothing bigger than a family of mice that had taken up residence in the kitchen cabinets. She was faintly surprised to find that, once inside, she could open the front door with a sturdy pull and step easily out onto the porch and back into the house without fanfare.

The second story was much like the first, a few bedrooms and a small bathroom with a tub guarded by a dusty plastic duck. Only one of the rooms gave Buffy pause. It was a boy's bedroom, if the blue sailboat wallpaper and matching bedspread were any indication. The closet and dresser still held clothing sized for a child of ten or twelve, but apart from a well-worn stuffed snake, none of the toys or games you would expect to find, nothing personal to the boy who had lived here, remained. Atop the dresser, however, was a small square patch directly in the center. The patch was unusual because it was the only surface in the entire house Buffy had seen that wasn't covered in at least an inch of dust.

Something was here, Buffy decided. *Something that was removed pretty recently.*

With her thumbs and forefingers, Buffy was able to measure and commit to memory the rough size of

the dustless square, and with only that much information, she left the house to its solitude and slow decay.
She considered waiting to see if Snyder would leave
the house the same way he'd entered, but it was almost
nightfall and the logic of the last few mornings suggested that the next time he would be roaming the
streets would be just before dawn.

Buffy knew she needed to set out in search of Callie, but now armed with proof that Snyder was perhaps
trafficking with the demon world, which might be
grounds for his termination—either from his job at the
high school or more permanently—Buffy decided to
check in on Willow first, to see if she'd made any
progress with her research.

"Good evening, Mrs. Rosenberg," Buffy said politely
when Willow's auburn-haired mother opened her front
door twenty minutes later. Buffy had considered first
searching for her friend at the school library, but
reminded herself that Willow was still under a strict
curfew and had probably returned home shortly after
she'd set off after Snyder, undoubtedly with piles of
take-home reading in her backpack.

"Oh, hello, Bunny," Mrs. Rosenberg replied
absentmindedly. Though it was hardly bedtime, Willow's mom was already wearing a fluffy cotton
bathrobe, and her demeanor was that of someone who
had been awakened from a sound sleep in the middle
of the night.

"I just stopped by to pick up some history notes
from Willow," Buffy said.

"All right"—Mrs. Rosenberg nodded—"but keep it brief." She stepped back to allow Buffy to enter.

"Brief is my middle name," Buffy said, and smiled as she headed upstairs, certain that from now on, Willow's mom would probably refer to her as Bunny Brief Summers. Mrs. Rosenberg, like Joyce, had a superhuman ability to rationalize and ignore the myriad strange things that had surrounded her daughter once she had become friends with Buffy. What never ceased to amaze Buffy and Willow were the odd and random facts that managed to stick, as well as those their mothers chose to care about. If, for example, Mrs. Rosenberg were ever to find out that Willow was now dating Oz, Buffy was pretty sure that the problem wouldn't be that he was both older than Willow and a werewolf; the difficulty Mrs. Rosenberg would have to overcome was the fact that he was in a band.

She found Willow in her room, seated on her full-size bed, surrounded by dozens of well-worn books. One of them was open in her lap, and though her head was bent forward as if she were reading it, Willow's soft, regular breathing told Buffy that her friend had dozed off. Looking past this adorable scene, Buffy felt a quick pull in her stomach as she noted that Willow's aquarium was still empty. A few weeks earlier Angel had sent the Slayer a warning in the form of killing Willow's fish. The only upside was that they were relatively new fish for Willow, and she hadn't even had a chance to name them before they had met their untimely end.

Knowing how exhausted Willow must be, Buffy

almost hesitated to wake her. Unfortunately, she had no choice.

"Wil?" Buffy said softly, gently nudging her friend.

In response, Willow's head snapped up with a snort.

"Oh, Buffy . . . what am I . . . I have to get home . . . ," she stammered.

"You *are* home, Willow," Buffy replied gently. "And I need your help."

Willow blinked her eyes rapidly and rolled her neck back until it clicked. She then put the kibosh on a huge yawn and, rubbing her eyes, said, "Did you find Callie?"

"Not yet," Buffy said, shaking her head. "I caught Snyder leaving campus early and decided to follow him."

Even tired Willow was intrigued. "You mean the principal was playing hooky?"

Buffy gave her the broad strokes of her trip to Arborville, and by the time she was done, Willow had already relocated to her computer and was pulling up any information she could find about the house in question.

Struggling between yawns, Willow did a quick search of the county tax files and a number of other databases that Buffy was certain weren't accessible to the public at large but thankfully were no match for Willow's hacking skills.

"Well . . . the house is in Snyder's name," she finally said.

"What does that mean?" Buffy asked. "It can't be his house. You know what a neat freak he is. The smell alone would give him hives."

"It's not his primary residence, at least according to the tax records," Willow continued. "He lives in a condo near the bluff. But he inherited this house fifteen years ago when his mother died. There are no records indicating that it was ever listed for sale after that."

"It's definitely a fixer-upper," Buffy said.

"I'm pretty sure it was the house he grew up in, though," Willow added. "It was originally purchased in the fifties by Thomas Snyder but he died not long after that, when Snyder was seven or eight, and it went to Snyder's mom, Paulina."

"So when do you think they installed the trick door?" Buffy asked.

Willow turned to her friend with a wince. "I don't think there's a permit you can pull for that kind of thing. Oh, wait . . ." Willow rose quickly and tossed a few of her reference books aside until she found what she was seeking.

"Don't tell me Giles has a book about demon home contractors," Buffy said.

"No . . . gateways," Willow replied, flipping pages. "They're barriers between our dimension and other dimensions."

"And I'm guessing that some of those gateways have demons behind them," Buffy said.

"Gateways are extremely rare," Willow continued. "Usually they're not static, and most often you have to be a demon to use them."

"Haven't I been saying for over a year that Snyder has to be a demon?" Buffy interrupted. "Between the attitude and the fashion sense . . . he's not fooling anyone. The man is evil."

"I know"—Willow nodded—"but before you slay him, we need to make sure that he's not being drawn to another dimension against his will."

"That would be less fun for me," Buffy acknowledged.

"Yes, but it's also possible," Willow said pointedly.

"So how do I use one of these gateways?" Buffy asked. "The thing wouldn't light up for me no matter what I did, and I have a bump on my head to prove it."

Willow did a little quick reading and finally arrived at a verdict. "Oh, gross," she said.

"What?" Buffy demanded.

Willow showed Buffy the text in question and read aloud: "'To gain access, a human must be either expected or invited. In the absence of an invitation, the blood of one who is invited may suffice to pass the barrier.'"

For the first time since they had started to piece the puzzle together, Buffy smiled.

"So I need to get some of Snyder's blood? And it's for a good cause?"

"Yes," Willow said, "but, Buffy . . ."

"I know." Buffy rolled her eyes. "I don't get to kill him unless I can prove beyond a shadow of a doubt that he's not just annoying but that he's really taken out a time-share with Satan. Still . . . this could be fun."

Willow closed the book and tossed it back on her

bed. "Are you going back there now, or are you going to look for Callie?" she asked.

"I don't imagine I'll have any luck tracking Snyder down until morning, so I'm Buffy the Vampire Hunter for now," she replied, then considered her friend's slumped shoulders and paler-than-normal complexion. "Why don't you get some sleep . . . or as much sleep as you can," she offered. "Have you had any luck with your theory on Sunnydale's sleeping sickness yet?"

Willow shook her head. "No. But I have to keep looking. This can't go on. Are you as tired as I am?"

Buffy thought about it for a minute. She had to admit that she was exhausted. But she'd been to the land of no-sleep many times before and so far she didn't seem much worse for the wear. *I guess that's just the luck of the Slayer,* she mused, though if she'd had her pick at the superpower store, this gift would have come well behind a number that she didn't possess, including the ability to force her mother to give her a car, or at least allow her to get a driver's license. Still, not wanting to rub it in, she replied, "Yeah. I could sleep for a month. But I'm not going to until we sort this out."

Willow nodded. "I think I'll make myself some coffee," she decided.

"Seriously, Wil," Buffy started to protest.

"No. My mind is made up. See my tired but determined face? Anyway, if I'm right, closing my eyes won't do any good."

"Okay." Buffy nodded. "Thanks for this, and I'll see you in the morning."

"Bright-eyed and bushy-tailed," Willow added. "Or maybe dark-circle-eyed and straggly tailed."

"Either way." Buffy smiled and gave her friend a quick hug before heading back downstairs.

On her way out, Buffy passed Mrs. Rosenberg asleep in front of the evening news.

I hope Willow's wrong about this, she thought as she let herself out the front door. Thing was, Willow was usually right, and if she was, the demon who was denying all of Sunnydale their sleepytime was going to move right to the top of Buffy's crap list. She honestly couldn't help thinking that the dice would come up Snyder.

Giles was accustomed to working all hours of the day and night. Obviously so were the pair of detectives who summoned him to a quaint suburban home several miles west of the school after ten o'clock in the evening. Unfortunately they needed no introduction. The first was a middle-aged man named Stein, who shook Giles's hand limply and offered a weak "Thanks for coming on such short notice." Giles vaguely remembered meeting Stein at the school a few months earlier, when the police had been investigating Buffy's assault on a man named Ted Buchanan. Though Buffy was never charged in the case, and Ted had turned out to be a homicidal robot, Giles still remembered darkly those few days when Buffy was devastated by the thought that she had harmed a human being.

Stein's partner in the current investigation was the clearly overworked Detective Winslow, an African-

American woman Giles had already had the pleasure of meeting when his past came back to haunt and try to kill him in the form of a demon called Eyghon.

On the one hand, Giles hated the idea that he was so well known among Sunnydale's law enforcement community. Rule one of being a Watcher was to keep a low profile. Rule two: See rule one. On the other hand, Giles had often wondered how oblivious those who were entrusted with securing the safety of a town situated on a Hellmouth could be to the supernatural phenomena that surrounded them. He had no proof, but his instincts told him that someone, somewhere had to know more than what was reported in the papers. It was much too convenient that vampire attacks were almost always described as "kids on PCP." It smacked of a cover-up that had to go higher than the flatfoots who worked Sunnydale's streets. Just how high, however, Giles did not know.

Giles had been at home when the call came. Though he wasn't convinced that Willow's theory about the strange sleeping sickness was on target, he had to admit that he was exhausted and had planned to make an early evening of it when he was roused by the late-night jangling of his phone. He'd rushed to answer it, assuming it would be Buffy, and was taken aback when Detective Stein advised him that they had found evidence of a crime that they believed Giles might be able to illuminate for them.

Twenty minutes later he was standing in the middle of a full-blown investigation. The house was surrounded by yellow police tape, and several portable lights had been brought in to aid the detectives who were searching the front and back yards for clues.

Giles's concern intensified when he noted the coroner's van pulled discreetly up between the police cars that lined the street in front of the house.

"We need you to take a look at this for us," Stein said simply as he ushered Giles through the foyer. Most of the activity seemed to be centered around the kitchen and an open doorway that probably led to the home's basement. Officers wearing protective clothing moved silently past the remains of a dinner table set for two, pausing occasionally to dust for fingerprints.

Stein led Giles, with Winslow trailing behind, away from the kitchen and down a dark hallway toward a bedroom. He paused outside the second doorway on the left and gestured for Giles to enter ahead of him.

Giles did so, still completely at a loss to understand what possible connection he might have to what appeared to be the room of a normal teenage boy. Giles quickly recognized many of the textbooks lined neatly on a small desk as those of a freshman year student. A number of various-size soccer trophies were arranged neatly on a shelf above the desk. The only odd thing, as far as Giles could tell, was the incredible neatness around him. Even he hadn't been this fastidious as a child.

A book bag hung on the back of the desk chair, and what Giles presumed were its contents had been neatly laid out on the perfectly made bed. As Winslow rather obviously studied Giles's face for any spark of recognition or interest, Stein moved past Giles to the bed and, with gloved hands, picked up a medium-size, well-worn leather book and offered it to Giles to examine.

"Does this look familiar to you?" Stein asked warily.

It did.

It was a copy from his private collection of Marc Leon's *Raising Demons*, a spellbook valued more for its detailed illustrations than the efficacy of its spells.

"There's a dedication inside the front cover," Winslow said, motioning to Stein to open the book. Stein complied and read, "'To Rupert Giles, best of luck with this one, signed Quentin Travers.'"

The book had been something of a joke between Giles and the man who now ran the Watchers Council. In younger days, both had been tested several times in the use of rather complicated spells that might serve in their work as Watchers. Quentin, who had never demonstrated Giles's skill with magicks, had been challenging Giles's abilities, certain that Leon's formulas were outdated at best.

Giles hadn't seen the book in months, but of course that meant nothing. Though he kept most of his private collection locked in the library's cage or in his office, the intensity of the research required of him in the last two years had made keeping track of such minor works less of a priority than he would have liked. Still, he couldn't imagine how it had ended up at this house.

"Mr. Giles?" Winslow interrupted his musings.

"Yes? Sorry," Giles said quickly. "The book is mine, as you've no doubt already surmised."

"A little light reading?" Winslow asked.

"It was actually what you might call a 'gag' gift," Giles said honestly.

"A gift from you to Joshua Grodin?" Stein asked.

"I'm sorry," Giles replied. "I don't know anyone by that name. It was a gift to me. I've never lent it to anyone."

"Joshua was a student at Sunnydale High," Winslow offered.

"Was?" Giles asked, though in his gut he already knew the answer.

"His body, and that of his father, Robert, were found this evening in the basement," Winslow continued. "They were obviously the victims of a brutal and vicious attack."

"Hell, they were practically ripped limb from limb," Stein said, and shuddered.

Given the potential results of a successful demon raising, Giles didn't have a hard time imagining the condition in which the bodies must have been found, though he did have difficulty believing that a novice could have successfully used Leon's book to raise anything resembling a demon. It was probable, however, that performing a ritual on the Hellmouth, even an inefficient one, had an exponentially better chance of success than if it were done in another location.

"I see," Giles said. "I'm terribly sorry to hear that." Turning his attention back to Stein, he asked, "May I?"

Stein nodded and handed the book to Giles. He

leafed through it for a moment, noting that a page had been turned down in a chapter devoted to Protection demons. Giles didn't necessarily want to know more, but duty demanded that he gather as much information as possible, for Buffy's sake. It was now highly likely that a new threat had arisen, and that Buffy would be the one to face it.

"Do you have any idea how that book came to be in Joshua's possession?" Winslow asked pointedly.

Giles shook his head. "I don't," he answered. "It's possible he meant to borrow it from the library and simply forgot to check it out."

"An interesting choice for a school library," Stein said.

"As I said, Detective, this was from my personal collection and might have inadvertently been mixed in with the rest of the stacks. Teenagers, as you know, have both active and vivid imaginations. Who knows why a boy Joshua's age might have found this book interesting. I'm afraid it's also possible that the book was mixed in with some other legitimate research materials and Joshua might not even have been aware it was in his possession," Giles finished.

Of course he was lying. The question was, did Stein or Winslow have the good sense to see that he was lying?

Both detectives studied him carefully as he made his best poker face. Their scrutiny was interrupted moments later by a male voice calling to Detective Stein from down the hall.

Giles followed Stein and Winslow back toward the

living room, where they were met by a flushed-faced young man in uniform who had obviously spent the last few hours digging through the area's garbage cans. He had collected in a small evidence box an assortment of items that included partially burnt candles, dried herbs and roots, and several rags that were covered in a dark red substance that was obviously blood.

Though Giles couldn't be sure what the detectives would make of this find, it clarified for him at least some of what had happened in this house. Someone, most likely Joshua, had in fact attempted to raise a demon. It was also quite possible that he had succeeded. Giles studied the house for telltale signs of recent demon activity, really nothing more complicated than obvious signs of destruction. Demons called to this plane from alternate dimensions usually didn't adjust immediately to their new surroundings. The wreckage should have been intense.

It wasn't. Apart from the book and the description of the basement, there was nothing to suggest that anything demonic had ever been in this house.

Giles was troubled. He asked quietly if there was anything further the detectives required from him, and though they requested that he make himself available for further questioning should the need arise, and promised to return the book to him as soon as possible, they had nothing further for him at the moment.

Though Giles wanted nothing more than to return home and get a few hours of much needed rest, he, like Buffy, knew that his responsibilities must come first. Instead of heading for his house, he left the Grodin home and returned to the school library. Pulling a few choice weapons from his storage cage and keeping them handy, he locked himself into his office and set to work, doing his best to find out what kind of new hell Joshua Grodin had just released on Sunnydale.

Todd couldn't believe what he was seeing. Buffy had taken him completely by surprise. Sure, she was gorgeous, and she was disarmingly easy to talk to. Usually a girl had to be more than easy on the eyes and reasonably witty to get his attention, though. He didn't like to be a brain racist, but the only girls he'd ever seriously fallen for had all been sharper than he was, *and that was saying something*. Buffy's brain trust, on the other hand, seemed seriously underfunded at first blush, but there was something there. It was hard to put his finger on, but it was in the neighborhood of a word Todd had never before applied to a girl under twenty.

Wisdom.

She obstinately kept her mind free of the facts and tools that made academic achievement possible, but there was something else taking up that brain space, a level of experience, perhaps, that belied her age. She seemed older than she was, as if she had lived more, if that was possible, than any other high school junior could or should have. It wasn't the information contained in her mind that was so alarmingly delightful; it was the way her mind worked, how she seemed to take personally the fact that a good man had betrayed his cousin to steal a kingdom, or how a turn of phrase from a Victorian poet could make her eyes well up once the metaphor had been explained. Her reaction to this newfound knowledge seemed to indicate that she was linking it to secrets locked deep within her, secrets she couldn't possibly have had a chance to learn at the age of seventeen.

She was a complete enigma to him. She was utterly intriguing. He'd found himself flirting with her before he could help himself, and even after only a few nights in her company had begun to imagine many more, once they were free of the burden of her final exams.

So what was his mystery woman doing trading punches with two men with bad skin, wearing strangely formal attire for a spring evening in the middle of a public playground?

Todd had actually stopped by Buffy's house fifteen minutes earlier. She hadn't returned his call from the morning, and he was half hoping that this lapse hadn't been intentional and that he'd find her there, appropriately apologetic and happy to see him and ready to spend a few hours with him, studying or talking. But her bedroom light had been off when he'd turned up the front walk, and her mother's car wasn't in the driveway. He had started walking over to the Bronze to see if she was with her friends, and only paused at the unmistakable sounds of violence from the other side of the wall that separated Rosewood Park from its street entrance.

Todd didn't plan on getting involved. He was a good citizen, but he didn't need to be a hero. He wasn't above a quick 911 call, though, and had turned through the side gate to see if that was in order.

A few meters from the thick of the fight, a young woman, probably not much older than Buffy, lay on the ground. Meanwhile, his student kicked, punched, dodged, and took blows that he was sure would have knocked him unconscious several times over. He debated making his presence known and seeing if he could lend a hand, but Buffy seemed to have things more than under control. For a few moments he lost sight of them as they moved behind a jungle gym. The next thing he knew, the sounds of punching and bone crunching ceased and Buffy emerged winded and alone.

She rushed quickly to the side of the other young girl and helped her to her feet. Todd ducked behind a tree as the two girls made their way to the gate and out of sight.

Shaken, confused, and he had to admit it, a little turned on, Todd rose to his feet and decided to cross to the main gate to make his exit so as to avoid any possibility of running into Buffy.

He needed to think, and possibly, a drink.

He'd read Buffy's academic file before accepting his assignment. He knew she had a history of delinquent behavior, but once they'd met, he'd found it impossible to square the profile with the person. Now, he was unhappy to find that everything he'd heard and read about Buffy was probably true.

Buffy thought she'd seen everything. But tonight had been a first. When she'd crossed through Rosewood

Park, hoping to catch a glimpse of Callie or Spike, she hadn't been terribly surprised to see two vampires. The thing that had topped the charts was the fact that the vampires had already found a victim, a girl Buffy vaguely recognized from the volleyball team, and instead of feeding off her like run-of-the-mill blood-suckers would, they were actually doing a Thunder Dome Death Match with each other over who had seen the girl first.

After confirming that the girl was just injured, and far from dead, Buffy had thrown herself into the fray. She had actually had a difficult time keeping the vampires away from each other and focused on her. She hadn't seen either of the two soon-to-be-dusters around, but she got the distinct impression that they weren't new to the whole suck-squad routine. This made it even harder to understand why they were wasting their time fighting each other over something they could have easily shared.

And then it struck her.

Just like Larry and Jonathan in the school cafe-teria.

It was a scary thought. Buffy paused before her closet door as she tossed her now bloodstained white tank blouse into the "Do Not Show Mom" pile, realizing that it was altogether possible that whatever was screwing with the living population of Sunnydale's sleep patterns might be affecting that of its undead residents as well.

Come to think of it, Slayer strength aside, Buffy had to acknowledge that she hadn't been at her sharpest in the evening's battle. She'd managed, of course, but she'd telegraphed too many punches and kicks, giving the vamps too much time to dodge or recover.

Once the fight was done, and Valerie the volleyball queen had been safely seen to her front door, Buffy had quickly decided that Callie and Spike would have to keep for another night. She hadn't even bothered with preparing speeches for Giles as she'd made her way back home. She'd walked in a daze, only certain of the fact that she intended to be up before dawn and back in Arborville to see what happened when whatever demon dimension had sucked Snyder in spat him back out again.

She really needed to get some rest. And she had a sinking feeling that tonight, once again, that wasn't going to happen. She set her alarm for an hour before sunrise and lay down to grab less than four hours of not too deep sleep.

The next thing she knew, it was morning. Her alarm had been going off for over two hours without waking her, and she had not only missed Snyder, but was about to be late for school.

Chapter Eight

Only once that Buffy was hurrying up the steps that led to the school's main entrance did she mentally slap herself upside the head, thinking, *Todd*. She was supposed to call him yesterday and she'd been so out of it when she got home that she hadn't even bothered to check her messages. Worst-case scenario, she was scheduled to see him the next afternoon, but she didn't want to waste the "I think he likes me" vibes she was already getting from him by flaking this early in the potential relationship. She also wanted to make sure that Angel hadn't killed him, or worse, turned him, but she wouldn't have a chance to do that until after school. The good news was, if he wasn't dead yet, there was little chance he would be before sundown.

Buoyed with these hopes, she rushed through the

main doors just as the second and final morning bell was shrilling through the halls.

The deserted halls.

The only sign she got that she hadn't shown up at school on a Saturday by mistake was running into Jonathan, who still stood at his locker despite the fact that classes had just begun. Unlike Buffy, however, Jonathan didn't seem to be troubled by his tardiness. He wasn't rushing.

No, he's not moving, Buffy realized.

Opening his locker a little wider, she saw his closed eyes and slack-jawed mouth and realized he was, like Joyce the previous morning, asleep on his feet.

She gently nudged him and received no response.

"Jonathan?" she said, and again louder, "Jonathan?"

Nothing.

She was contemplating a good solid slap to wake him when a bone-chilling scream echoed through the otherwise empty hall. She quickly turned to see Cordelia running toward the girls' restroom a few yards down shrieking and scratching at her arms and neck.

Buffy hurried into the bathroom after her and found her at the sink, splashing water all over her arms and shouting, "Get them off me! Get them off!"

"Cordelia," Buffy said, grabbing her and checking her arms for good measure. Buffy wasn't a doctor but they looked like normal healthy bare arms, apart from the welts starting to rise where Cordelia had already scratched herself deeply enough to leave marks.

"Get them off!" Cordelia screamed louder.

"Get *what* off?" Buffy said, matching her tone and holding Cordelia's arms down to keep her from further harming herself.

For a second, Cordelia's eyes finally focused on Buffy, and she was surprised to see a flash of relief in them. She knew that she and Cordy were never going to be BFF, but there was something gratifying in knowing that her mere presence could calm Cordelia down.

"Oh, Buffy," she said, dazed. "Spiders . . ."

But as the words trailed off, Cordelia abruptly lost consciousness and fell to the floor.

Okay, this is ridiculous, Buffy decided.

She was tempted to pick her up and carry her to her next stop, the library, but quickly decided that, in this case, it wouldn't do Cordelia any permanent damage to stay where she was until Buffy figured out what was going on and how to kill it.

Moments later she rushed into the library, calling out, "Giles!" but the only response came from Willow, who was seated at the main table surrounded by stacks of books four feet high in every direction.

"Buffy . . . finally," Willow said weakly.

Concern trumped curiosity at the sight of her friend, bleary eyed and struggling to remain conscious.

Buffy hurried to the table, grabbed Willow by the shoulders, and examined her condition. Her breath was shallow and ragged. She was paler than usual, and she struggled with every blink to keep her dry and bloodshot eyes open.

"Willow, what is it?" Buffy demanded.

"Can't fall asleep . . . ," Willow said.

"Okay," Buffy said in her most reasonable voice. "Why not?"

"Won't wake up," Willow said, pushing Buffy aside and, staggering behind the library counter, downed a few gulps the remains of what had to be at least a day-old cup of coffee.

The good news was this seemed to fortify her a bit, for the moment. Buffy could only pray that the coffee in question had at least once belonged to Giles, because anything else was too yick to contemplate.

"I think I figured it out," Willow said more firmly as she rejoined Buffy at the table.

"You have my undivided attention," Buffy replied.

"It's a spell," Willow began. "And it's caused by a demon."

"This, I can work with," Buffy replied. "Just point me in the right direction and I'll kill the rest."

"The sleep deprivation is only the first part," Willow said. "None of us have really slept in days."

"Right," Buffy nodded. "I've already seen the trailer to this movie."

"Instead, we're experiencing what's called 'the sleep of living death.'"

"Wait a minute," Buffy said. "Where have I heard of that before?"

"It's like a trance," Willow continued. "Everyone affected loses consciousness, like when you sleep, but you're not really sleeping."

"So the demon in question is putting everyone in a trance so it can swoop down and, what? Eat our brains? Steal our socks? What does the demon want?" Buffy asked.

"I don't think it's meant for everyone," Willow said, pulling out one of her reference books and handing it to Buffy. "I found this legend about a town in France that fell asleep for a hundred years."

"*The Ice Capades*!" Buffy said with enthusiasm.

"Huh?" Willow had to ask.

"They did a really cool version of 'Sleeping Beauty on Ice' a few years ago. My dad and I went."

"Huh?" Willow repeated.

"That's the story where I heard about the sleep of living death thingie. Doesn't the spell put the whole kingdom to sleep for, like, a hundred years?"

"Buffy!" Willow said as sharply as she could through the grogginess.

"Right, sorry," Buffy said, chagrined. "Focusing now."

"This story predates any of the known sources for *Sleeping Beauty* or any other fairy tale by hundreds of years. In fact, it's very likely that this story might have been the inspiration for the tale that was eventually made famous by the Brothers Grimm. I've always thought their stories, though well told, were incredibly derivative, and just because they got all the credit—"

"Um, Willow?" Buffy interrupted. "Stay on target."

"Oh, sorry," Willow said, shaking her head to clear it. "The legend is about a farmer who angered a demon."

"How?" Buffy asked.

"He had pledged his best cow in return for a good yield on his crops and when the time came, he never paid up."

"It's almost hard to believe no one ever made an animated film about that one," Buffy said.

"So the demon cast a spell over the whole town, only it wasn't about the villagers. It was designed to put the farmer into a highly suggestive trance-state so that each night, the demon could draw the farmer into his dimension, where he was tortured mercilessly until sunrise."

"Wait, let me guess," Buffy interjected. "He brought the farmer to his dimension through a gateway?"

"Yes." Willow nodded. "This happened night after night, for more than a week. The farmer didn't have any memory of what happened to him in the demon-dimension. The problem was what happened to the rest of the town. The first part, we already know: People got agitated, then really cranky, and eventually they started trying to sleep at inappropriate times of the day because their bodies were literally shutting down. If you try to go long enough without sleep, eventually your body will make you sleep, or worse."

"So where's the 'worse'?" Buffy asked. "I thought sleep is what we all need right now."

"Yeah, but the villagers who fell asleep while under the spell didn't just sleep. They fell into the sleep of living death, from which no one could wake them," Willow replied.

"Until when?" Buffy asked.

"Until forever," Willow said.

"Okay," Buffy said thoughtfully, "so what about the prince and the dragon and the happily ever after part of the story?"

Even exhausted Willow had the presence of mind to roll her eyes at this one. "Buffy, how many times do we have to talk about fairy tales and propaganda?" she asked pointedly.

"Okay, so if you're right, the farmer in our scenario is Principal Snyder. I get some of his blood, I use it to go through the gateway. I find the demon and I kill it. That will stop the spell, right?" Buffy asked.

"No, the gateway is actually the key," Willow replied. "The spell emanates from the demon dimension that is linked to ours via the gateway. . . ." she trailed off.

It was clear that, despite the restorative powers of day-old caffeine, Willow was once again starting to fade.

"Willow?" Buffy said with genuine concern.

"Sorry. As long as the gateway exists, the spell will still bleed out into Sunnydale. It will remain open until that which was stolen is returned," Willow continued, reading a passage from her text as she pointed it out to Buffy.

"You lost me," Buffy said. "What was stolen?"

"I don't know," Willow said, frustrated. "In the legend, the demon stole something of the farmer's and used it to open the gateway in the first place. The only way to break the spell is to close the gateway, and the only way to do that is to find what the demon took from Snyder and bring it back with you."

Suddenly Buffy remembered the small dust-free patch on the dresser she'd found in the house.

"I think I might know what we're looking for," Buffy said. "Or at least its shape and size. I have to go back to the house. How long before everyone falls into this sleeping-death thing?" she asked.

"It depends," Willow replied. "If you were pretty well rested before it started, that would buy you some time. But . . ."

"From the looks of things around here, time has already started to run out," Buffy finished for her. "Have you discussed any of this with Giles?" was her next question.

Willow shook her head. "I haven't seen him this morning. I came in pretty early, once I found the legend at home. I wanted to cross-check it with the other sources . . . ," she said, struggling to keep her eyes open.

Buffy quickly scanned the library for any sign of Giles. The door to his office was locked, but that wasn't unusual when he wasn't present. Opting for the most efficient solution, she turned the knob hard, breaking the lock, and pushed open the door, where she was immediately met with the sight of Giles, collapsed on the office floor, holding a crossbow at his chest, pointed directly at the door.

Buffy knelt beside him and deftly extricated his fingers from the crossbow, then shook Giles a few times in a vain effort to wake him. Even after a good sharp slap across the face, for which she was sure he would forgive her—*he's certainly endured worse dur-*

ing our many training sessions—Giles could not be roused. Now more frightened than anything, Buffy returned to the main table where Willow sat dazed but still fighting to stay awake.

"Willow," Buffy said sharply, "I don't care what you have to do, you keep those peepers open."

"I'm trying," she said weakly, her head drooping forward.

"Willow!" Buffy said more firmly.

Willow's head snapped up, but at that moment their attention was drawn to the library door, which was thrown open by an incoherent, pajama-clad Xander.

"She's after me! Stop her!" he cried out in alarm, rushing to Buffy and cowering behind her.

Buffy immediately moved to check the door, but the hallway outside the library remained deserted. When she turned back, Xander had hidden himself under the table and seemed to be trying to barricade himself in with stacks of books, fortified by chairs.

"Xander!" Buffy demanded. "Stop with the building blocks and tell me what happened."

"All I did was grab a piece of toast," Xander insisted, the fear in his voice rising to a fever pitch. "It's toast. Not a federal crime. Why would she make the toast if she didn't want me to eat it?"

Buffy exchanged a worried glance with Willow, who seemed to have perked up a bit at Xander's entrance.

"Xander, I don't understand," Buffy said, her exasperation rising.

"I grabbed the toast, and suddenly she was going after my fingers with the butcher knife," Xander replied with what would have been an appropriate amount of terror in a five-year-old girl.

"Who?" Buffy asked.

"Mommy!" Xander shouted. He paused, searching his memory for a moment, then added, "At least it was my mommy at first."

"Xander, I don't understand," Buffy said, beginning to pull some of the books away from the barricade to get closer to her friend and hopefully calm him a bit.

"It was mom, and then it wasn't," he said, as if he were just as confused as Buffy. "It was my mom, and then it was a pig. A little pig. A pig that spoke English. It was angry with me because it said I had eaten it, but I never ate a pig. Well, there was that one time, but that wasn't really me, was it? Buffy, you have to kill that pig!"

Buffy turned to Willow, who was shaking her head.

"He's delirious," she said, answering Buffy's unspoken question. "He's hallucinating, taking stuff from his subconscious and confusing it with reality. It comes with the no sleeping."

"With a side of paranoia, I'm assuming," Buffy added.

Buffy didn't need a psychology course to understand the symbolism. A year earlier, Xander had briefly been possessed by a hyena demon, along with a pack of other students, and one of their most disgusting acts had been eating Sunnydale High's first and only living mascot alive.

Then she remembered Cordelia and the bathroom and the imaginary spiders. She also remembered how quickly Cordelia had collapsed after doing battle with her spiders.

"Xander," Buffy said in her most conciliatory tone, "don't worry about the pig. The pig can't get you here. You're safe."

Unfortunately, Xander had already lost consciousness behind the walls of his makeshift fort.

"Xander, wake up!" Buffy shouted.

He didn't respond. Like Giles, he was now one of the sleeping dead.

Buffy's heart started to race. Most of the really scary stuff she did as a Slayer, she did alone, but that didn't mean she wasn't both fortified and secured by the presence of her friends and their constant support. One by one, she was losing those she held most dear. Part of her demanded that she suck it up and get moving, while another part, the part that was still grieving the loss of Angel, demanded that she give in to her own fear and curl up in a tiny ball next to Xander until the danger had passed.

The problem was, the danger would never pass if she didn't pull herself together and go out and kick the danger's ass.

Forcing her fear and abandonment issues aside, she turned again to Willow, who was still seated at the table, but with her head tipped back and snoring softly.

Oh, and I was so close to not panicking, Buffy thought.

This ends now, she decided. She knew she would ultimately accept the loss of her first love. But strong as she was, she didn't think there would ever be a time or place when she could also resign herself to the loss of Willow, Xander, or Giles.

It was time to do what she did best.

It was time to be the Slayer.

Chapter Nine

First things first, Buffy thought as she squared her shoulders and walked briskly toward the library doors.

I need to find Snyder.

Buffy had no doubt he was the target of the demon, as he was the only person who seemed to be able to enter the gateway at will. She tried to imagine what in the world the demon would have stolen to draw him there. The legend didn't seem to indicate that it needed to be anything particularly meaningful to the victim, but Buffy firmly believed that whatever had once rested alone on the top of the chest of drawers in that little boy's bedroom had been a most prized possession. Given its size, it could have been a packet of Chicklets, or maybe more like a Rubik's Cube. Of course, they didn't have Rubik's Cubes a hundred years ago, or whenever it was that the principal had actually been a child. That fad had only started a few years before Buffy's birth; never mind the fact that Buffy seriously doubted that Snyder would ever have been able to solve the thing on his own.

Whatever it was would be found in the demon dimension on the other side of the gateway. She'd never actually been to a demon dimension, but in her imagination, anything brought over from her world would probably clash with the fires and chains and severed body parts and would hopefully be pretty easy to spot.

Buffy wanted to find Snyder immediately and force him through the gateway. The sooner the spell was broken, the sooner things would return to the abnormal state she had come to think of fondly as normal. She started with his office. Though most of the school was deserted, she allowed herself a fleeting hope that something might go her way and she'd find him there, but no luck. The office was empty.

Though she usually preferred to leave the Nancy Drew'ing to Giles and Willow, she did spend a few minutes looking around. She'd always hated this office, mainly because every time she'd ever been there, she'd been on the receiving end of Snyder's witless ranting. She wasn't surprised at all to find that her file was on top of his desk in a wire basket he'd marked "Beyond Hope," along with the files of several other students Buffy only knew by reputation as destined to spend the better part of their adult lives as guests of the state's penal institutions. She wasn't sure if the red and silver star stickers that Snyder had placed on her file next to her name were a good sign, but she seriously doubted it.

His desk was filled with your basic office supplies, though they were meticulously organized. It was in the rear of one of the lower file drawers where she found something that definitely gave her pause. Tossed behind a series of file folders were several days' worth of white bandages soaked generously with dried blood.

Oh, yuck.

Buffy didn't know if the blood she was going to need to go through the gateway had to be fresh, but just in case, she tucked a snippet of bandages into her pocket and immediately refused to think further about how thoroughly disgusting it was to have them anywhere near her.

The only other interesting discovery was a heavy stain on the carpet beneath Snyder's desk. A guy who arranged the pencils in his drawer by sharpness and length wasn't one to tolerate an obvious stain. Buffy had seen enough blood, dried and otherwise, to guess pretty quickly that here was more Snyder blood. The important thing to note was that it was fairly recent.

Obviously whatever games the demon is playing with Snyder each night must include some serious pain for him to be bleeding all over the carpet each day, Buffy thought without too much concern for the principal.

Buffy wished she had made note of the condo Snyder owned that Willow had identified as his permanent residence. Odds were, he was probably collapsed there, like most of the rest of Sunnydale by now. But given the demon's interest in him, Buffy doubted that this would be enough to stop him from keeping his evening date with the gateway.

With hours before he would make his appearance in Arborville, Buffy decided that between now and then she would do well to stock up on a few supplies from her weapons locker at home. Only now did it dawn on her that nothing Willow had told her gave her any clue about the demon she would be facing soon enough or how best to kill it.

I'll probably just use whatever's handy, she decided, wondering for the first time what demonic torture devices would look like. She had just started training with a really cool mace, a long silver shaft with a head of pointed spikes, and decided that that, plus several stakes and a small ax, would be the best accessories to complete her ensemble for the evening. She hurried back to collect the mace from Giles's personal weapons storage cage and then turned her steps toward Ravello Drive, where she'd find the rest of her things.

Walking the streets of Sunnydale midmorning, Buffy found her spirits sinking as she got a visceral feel for the impact of the sleep spell. Every business she passed was either empty or closed. The only cars she saw were parked, and a few contained drivers who might have tried to set off for work that morning but had finally succumbed to their own exhaustion and were now passed out in their seats. There was no traffic, not even the faint roar of engines a few streets away. It was the feeling Buffy usually associated with walking these same streets in the middle of the night, but the bright sunlight was jarring and dissonant.

As she turned off the main street and passed another car, still running with the driver collapsed over the armrest into the passenger's seat, she realized that she was going to have to end this thing well before nightfall, or as soon after as possible. If, as she suspected from her fight the night before, Sunnydale's undead population was also affected by the spell, the townspeople were safe for the time being. But if last night had just been a case of two vampires too stupid to live, then come sundown, the town might as well hang a sign saying "Smorgasbord" at the city's entrance. All of these defenseless people would be a vampire's Suck-a-palooza, and Buffy shuddered at the thought.

Nearing her home, she noticed that the suburban streets shooting off from the town's main thoroughfares were a little more clogged with early morning traffic. Of course, the traffic wasn't moving. A few people had left their cars and collapsed on the sidewalks. In the distance Buffy clearly heard a man screaming at the top of his lungs. She started to run toward the source of the shouting, but the minute the man caught sight of Buffy, he started to run in the other direction, still screaming something about "killer kumquats." Buffy decided he was, like the others, probably hallucinating and only moments away from dropping.

Hurrying up her front walk, Buffy noted that her mother's jeep was still in the driveway. Rushing inside, she called out, "Mom!" but received no answer. She finally found Joyce curled up on the bathroom floor, still holding her toothbrush, and with a few dribbles of toothpaste caked on her mouth. Though she knew it was probably useless, she tried to wake her mother. Her pulse once again doing the mambo, she lifted Joyce carefully and took her back into her bedroom, arranged her on the bed as comfortably as possible, and wiped her hands and face with a wet washcloth. Though her mother looked peaceful enough as she slept, Buffy couldn't shake the overwhelming desire to try to force her mother to wake up.

Strange to be the handsome prince who gets to slay the dragon and wake the princess with a kiss in this scenario, she thought. *Just once, I wouldn't mind being the rescued.*

With a deep sigh, Buffy hurried to her room, grabbed the last few things she needed, and set out for the Snyder house.

All she could do until he arrived was wait.

Buffy hated waiting.

"For God's sake, either kiss her or kill her," Spike said aloud to the television screen, frustrated that, once again, the producers of *Sunset Beach* seemed determined to draw out the "will they or won't they?" question for Annie and Gregory until he was well past caring. He knew the chaps who wrote this twaddle were just doing their job, but seriously, if these two didn't start shagging soon so that Olivia could come in and find them and—*wishful thinking*—cut them both into tiny pieces for their betrayal, he was going to have to find a new daytime drama.

There was little else to do when the sun was up. Spike didn't think of himself as high maintenance. He didn't need much sleep, and though he was definitely much wearier than usual this morning, he rarely turned in for a little rest until his programs were over. Give him Drusilla, a few hours of telly, and a little fresh blood each day and he was a happy man.

Though he had to admit that little Callie was also quickly becoming something that he wasn't sure he wanted to live without. He cast a quick glance in her direction and satisfied himself that she was still humming softly to herself on the sofa as she whittled the hours away.

Thankfully, feeding time was no longer an issue. Once Callie'd had her first taste of human blood, she'd been a new girl. He would forever treasure the look on that snotty little Michael's face when Callie had jumped him from behind and sunk her little fangs into his neck. That had been passion. She'd sucked him well past dry and, turning to Spike, her face aglow and Michael's fresh blood still dripping from her lips, had screamed, "More, Daddy!"

Adam had come next. Only the sounds of approaching sirens had stopped Spike from turning her loose on the entire team and their coaching staff. What the hell was T-ball supposed to be, anyway? There simply wasn't a sport that Americans couldn't find a way to muck up.

He and his little pet would be hunting again tonight. *After I've caught a quick nap,* Spike decided. Callie had set her sights on a young girl named Amanda who had once teased her for weeks at a time for having the audacity to wear little pink bows at the ends of her braids, and this was a sin for which Amanda must pay dearly.

He was grateful that Callie had yet to ask him any questions about the birds and vampire bees. It didn't seem to have occurred to her yet to wonder where vampires came from, or to want to sire any herself. Frankly, he preferred it this way. He didn't really want to share Callie right now with anyone but Drusilla, who had expressed more than once her delight in the changes Spike was bringing about with their child. Callie had even taken to spending the occasional few minutes with her mommy, playing nicely with her dolls. They were becoming something resembling a happy family, just the three of them, and thankfully, Angelus seemed too preoccupied with Buffy and someone called Todd to bother them much.

In fact, if all went as well as Spike hoped this evening, it was altogether possible that none of them would be troubled by Angelus at all in the near future.

It hadn't totally been Spike's doing. Though Callie didn't seem concerned with the birth of a new vampire, they had discussed at some length those things, including a pair of Slayers named Buffy and Kendra, that could hurt or kill a vampire. Until Spike was certain that Callie was either strong enough to hold her own in a fight or cunning enough to know when to run, he was going to make sure that she and the Slayer from hell never crossed paths. But once Callie had learned that vampires were kill-able, she had begun to ask many leading questions about their housemate, Angelus.

Callie didn't like Angelus. The "time-out" had been a huge mistake, and Callie had apparently decided then and there that the world wouldn't miss Angelus much. So, with Spike's permission, she wondered if she might not be allowed to kill him.

Normally, Spike would have resisted. He knew full well that demons often killed other demons, but once a bond had been forged between them like the one that bound Spike to Drusilla and Dru to Angelus, killing out of spite was simply not done. *Unless I am absolutely certain I can get away with it.*

Spike wasn't going to be starting an "I Love Angelus" fan club any time soon either. Though he wasn't planning to deal the death blow himself— *there'd be ten kinds of hell to pay with Dru*—he didn't see the harm in staying out of Callie's way.

"What do you think, Spikey?" Callie asked sweetly, holding up the little stake she'd been carving for hours.

Spike tested the pointy end himself and managed to prick his finger with it. "Very nice work, pet," he replied with a smile.

"Can I do it now? Please, please, please?" she asked.

Spike hadn't seen Dru or Angelus since last sundown.

For all he knew, they were hiding out in the sewers after a long night of hunting.

I guess it wouldn't hurt to look, though, he decided.

"Climb on up, then." Spike nodded, and Callie crawled onto his lap.

As they rolled down the main hall toward Angelus's suite of rooms, Callie hummed contentedly to herself.

"What's that you're singing, love?" Spike asked softly.

"One of these things is not like the others," Callie sang softly in his ear. *"One of these things just doesn't belong. Can you tell me which one is not like the others, before I have time to finish . . ."*

"That would be Angelus," Spike whispered back, wondering again why he was so bloody tired this morning.

Callie rewarded him with a bright smile. "Daddy Spike always knows," she said happily.

That he does, love. That he does.

Any vague doubts he might have been nursing were silenced when they finally found Angelus. He wasn't in his room, or the dining hall, or anywhere else in the living areas. Spike had almost despaired of their chances, when a bleak thought had stuck in his gut, a thought too troubling to dismiss.

He wouldn't, Spike told himself.

But then, this was Angelus. That phrase almost never applied to him.

They'd found Angelus, just as Spike had feared, in Drusilla's bed. Had he been alone, Spike might have killed him then and there just for being so cheeky.

But he wasn't.

Angelus lay on his side, curled up beside Spike's beloved Dru, both of them sleeping deeply. And the worst part: Dru was smiling in her sleep.

Spike swallowed his rage.

"Go ahead, then, little bit," he whispered to Callie. Part of him wanted this moment for himself. He'd been looking forward to a good knock-down, drag-out with the bastard since Angelus first joined them, once again soul-free just after Drusilla had reassembled The Judge. But this had been Callie's plan, and part of him wanted to see her succeed. It was a gift he was giving her, a new side of the powers that lived within her that she would only now begin to explore in all their glory. Once Angelus was out of the way, he, Dru, and Callie would kick the dust of Sunnydale from their feet and go elsewhere—Europe, South America, anywhere but here.

And then, what games we'll play, he thought with a smile.

Callie gave Spike a quick pat on his head.

"Stay here, Daddy," she said. Then she crawled off his lap and, with slow, delicate motions, began to make her way in between Angelus and Dru.

Spike saw her clear the space and noted with relief that neither Angelus nor Dru even stirred. Callie turned back to smile at Spike, then raised her pale little hand, holding the business end of her stake pointed directly at Angelus's heart.

That was the last thing Spike remembered as the blackness took him.

Buffy felt like she'd been waiting forever. In fact, it had only been a few hours. As the afternoon sun had started to wind its way down in the sky, she'd found slivers of shade beneath the branches of the jacaranda tree near the edge of the front porch. She was grateful she'd thought to bring a few diet sodas with her for her little stakeout. Though she was far from dropping in her tracks, she was certainly feeling the burn of past several sleepless nights, and sitting around waiting was almost as much fun as watching Giles reorganize his ancient reference book collection.

As the sun dipped toward the horizon, casting longer shadows down the row of dilapidated houses, Buffy started to worry that perhaps Snyder, like the others, had succumbed to "the sleep of living death" and might not show up. She'd toyed with the idea of using the bandages in her pocket to try to enter the gateway on her own, but even if she found the demon and killed it, she didn't relish the idea of searching an entire other dimension for the object that would close the gateway and break the spell. For all she knew, the demon had parents, or babies, or groupies, and once she crossed over, she could be lost there for days, years, or even the rest of her life if something went really wrong. At least she knew that Snyder could find his way out, and though some of the potential scenarios she had imagined that afternoon included his untimely death *at the hands of the demon, of course*, she both hoped and feared that once the big nasty had been disposed of, Snyder would be able to lead her back to the gateway.

If the sun set completely, she would have no choice. With or without the principal, she was going in. She rose to stretch and started to pace the length of the front yard, changing her mind with every minute that passed about just how long she would wait for Snyder to show.

Finally, a few minutes after six, by her watch, a loping shadow approached. With the sun behind him, the figure was shrouded in darkness, but the outline, from the balding head and unmistakable ears, as well as the definite limp, told her that, finally, her quarry had arrived.

As expected, Snyder took no notice of Buffy. He walked in a daze, a faint smile playing across his lips. Tonight, along with his uniform suit, he was wearing a pair of open-toed sandals. Buffy took a moment to imagine Snyder in the shorts and probably Hawaiian-print shirt he might have bought these sandals for, and couldn't help shaking her head. She doubted the man knew the meaning of relaxation, let alone how one might go about getting some. She also noted that the toes of his left foot were covered in blood-soaked bandages. He was leaving a fresh trail behind him with every step.

Without a glance in Buffy's direction, Snyder walked straight up the front path and disappeared in a flash of light through the front door. She followed his steps to the porch and, for good measure, removed the fouled bandages from her pocket and dabbed them in the blood Snyder had left as he passed the spot. Taking a deep breath and clasping her weapons bag firmly in her right hand, she walked again toward the front door and, instead of meeting any resistance, suddenly found herself surrounded by a burning white light.

The next sight that met her eyes wasn't at all what she had expected.

Chapter Ten

Buffy thought she'd had time to prepare herself. She'd imagined the dimension where Snyder would be tortured nightly, and frankly, she was hoping for something grim. The best mental picture she'd been able to concoct had been something akin to the basement beneath the University of California-Sunnydale fraternity house where she and Cordelia had bonded several months earlier while chained to the stone walls in preparation for being fed to a giant snake named Mikida. Add a little fire and brimstone, or maybe a river of blood, and the picture would be complete.

She hadn't been prepared to cross into her very first demon dimension and find herself in the entryway to a house that looked like it was sold to the Snyders by June and Ward Cleaver.

It was, in fact, the exact house she had searched

the evening before, minus the dust and cobwebs and the stench that reminded her of her grandmother's closet. To her left was the living room. The sofa looked like it had been shrink-wrapped, but upon closer examination, Buffy realized that the cushions were simply slip-covered with plastic. The same "Home Sweet Home" pillow whose sad abandon she had lingered over before looked positively perky, giving the otherwise bland room a splash of festive color.

Buffy could have eaten off of the coffee table, the surface was so clean. In fact, every piece of furniture had been dusted and polished to within an inch of its life. Though the wood paneling that ran the length of the far wall only vaguely resembled real wood, it glowed with a warm sheen that only hours of elbow grease and a rag could have produced.

The front window that Buffy had unceremoniously broken the first time she had entered the house was intact, and framed with slightly yellowed lace curtains that had certainly once been white. The faded color was not a product of neglect. The curtains actually looked freshly ironed. It was their age that betrayed them.

To the right of the entryway, Buffy saw the dining room table, still adorned with its arrangement of fake apples, bananas, and grapes, still covered by a freshly pressed peach linen cloth, minus the moth holes. Taking better inventory of the dining room, Buffy noted an antique china cabinet that housed a complete collection, up through the mid 1960s, of presidents of the United States dinner plates. Each was boldly etched with the name and years of service, along with a truly frightening portrait of Herbert Hoover, Theodore Roosevelt, and Grover Cleveland, among all the others.

A swinging door separated the dining room from the kitchen, at least if the savory smells of a home-cooked dinner that set Buffy's stomach rumbling were any indication. Listening closely, Buffy was almost sure that she heard a faint and pleasant humming coming from the other side.

Buffy returned to the entry hall and saw Snyder reach the landing at the top of the staircase and turn to his left, toward what Buffy knew was the little boys' room she'd searched before. To her surprise, there was a definite spring in his step. At the very least, he no longer appeared to be limping.

Torn between facing whatever was in the kitchen and making sure she had a chance to find the all-important stolen object, Buffy opted to follow Snyder. As quietly as possible, she crossed the hall and tiptoed up the stairs.

A few steps down the upstairs hall, Buffy noted a swash of light spilling out from the first bedroom. Cautiously, she crept toward it. Though the door was slightly ajar, Buffy had to push it open another few inches to really get a good look at the room.

Snyder stood with his back to Buffy near the open closet. He was removing his sandals and lining them up neatly with what appeared to be several other pairs of fully grown-man-size shoes. Flabbergasted, Buffy realized that Snyder's toes were no longer covered in bloody bandages. In fact, his bare feet looked positively healthy as he wriggled his toes in the deep beige pile carpet.

Buffy did a quick check of the carpet in the hall and stairs and satisfied herself that Snyder was no longer leaving a trail of blood behind him. Whatever damage was done to him in this place didn't seem to affect him until he re-entered the real world. Willow had seemed so sure about the being tortured part, but apart from the 1950s suburban nightmare décor, Buffy could see little that would cause anyone, least of all Snyder, any pain here.

Taking a deep breath, Buffy opened the bedroom door wide enough to enter. She fervently hoped that, just as before, Snyder would take no notice of her, and at first he did just that. The principal sat cross-legged on his bed, one arm wrapped around the stuffed snake that was now restored to its full glory in a plush pattern of orange and yellow diamonds, absentmindedly stroking it with one hand while the other nimbly turned the pages of a comic book resting in his lap.

Buffy turned immediately toward the dresser, whose surface she could only see once she'd entered, and with a triumphant smile saw that standing in its center was a small trophy. A golden bee rested atop a small wooden base, almost certainly the exact size of the dust square she'd committed to memory. Buffy moved closer and peered in to read the inscription on the plaque attached to the trophy's base: "Cecil Snyder, 5th place, Arborville Elementary School Spelling Bee."

She honestly didn't know what was more shocking, the idea that this little trophy might be so prized by her principal that he would have displayed it so prominently, or that his first name was Cecil.

Suddenly, Cecil's face was next to hers. "That Bobby Matthews thought he was so tough, but I sure showed him, didn't I?" he said, the exuberance on his face a clear indication that Bobby, whoever he was, hadn't cracked the top five in the spelling bee.

"You sure did?" Buffy replied, unsure how to proceed.

Cecil smiled warmly at her as he gently picked up the trophy, blew on it to create some condensation, then rubbed it vigorously with his shirtsleeve. Once he was satisfied with the faint gleam of the fake bronze leaf, he restored it to its place of honor, nudging it slightly a few times to make sure its position was perfect.

"So . . . um . . . ," Buffy began, wondering when he was going to demand to know what she was doing in his bedroom and begin to describe in detail the many ways he was now going to expel her.

His next question came out of the blue, even more so than the last comment, if that was possible.

"Do you like comic books?" he asked sweetly.

Okay, am I on "Demon Candid Camera?" Buffy thought. She was starting to wonder if all of this—the gateway, the house that looked like a set from *Leave It to Beaver*, and, most of all, "Cecil"—was some kind of demon practical joke.

Maybe demons don't have cable and this is what they do for fun.

Cecil was waiting expectantly for an answer. When she didn't respond right away, he dashed over to his bed and lifted the mattress from the box spring to reveal dozens of comics, most of which looked like they'd been read and reread many times.

"I've got *Denizens of the Dead, I Was a Teenage Zombie, The Creature Within*—only volumes three through seven, though. Once the creature gets his heart back and starts going all lovey-dovey with Miss Constance, I think the story really goes downhill, don't you? Oh, and I also have the very first edition of *The Ascendant*—have you heard of that one yet? It's pretty new."

Buffy's head started to spin. She hated this man. He had never once been anything less than horrible to her. He'd taken every bit of power entrusted in him by the school board and wielded it toward his own perverse little ends. Human or not, he *was* evil. What began to dawn on her through the haze was the fact that he hadn't always been the man she knew. Once, many, many years ago, he had been little Snyder. He had been Cecil, in a bedroom with sailboat wallpaper, and with a best friend who was a stuffed snake.

Once, Snyder had been a child.

And apparently, once wasn't enough.

To all intents and purposes, the man who had terrorized every moment of her school life for the past year, starting with his insistence that she, Willow, and Xander humiliate themselves at the school talent show, and including the parent-teacher night for which he'd made her create posters and refreshments so that he could corner Joyce and share with her his conviction that Buffy belonged in a juvenile detention facility rather than on his campus, had vanished. He stood before her barefoot, but still wearing his brown pin-stripe suit and black clip-on tie, every last inch an adult, but with the mentality of a ten-year-old boy.

Take a moment and marvel at the incongruity.

Okay. Marveling done.

Cecil was still waiting for an answer. Buffy moved closer to the bed and took a good look at his comic book collection. In one sense, it wasn't disappointing. Apparently, even as a small child his tastes had leaned toward the dark side. Image after image of hell-demons mutilating humans, brain-eating zombies, and something that looked vaguely like a half-man, half-giant spider assaulted her eyes. That had to be a sign of something, right?

Maybe it would be more disturbing if he spent his time reading Pat the Bunny, Buffy had to admit.

"Um . . . Cecil," Buffy said hesitantly.

"If you don't like comic books, that's cool," Cecil said, closing the mattress lid on his treasure-trove. "A lot of girls I know aren't into them."

"You know a lot of girls?" Buffy couldn't help but ask.

"Oh, sure." Cecil shrugged, obviously trying to play it down. "There's Marsha, who has had a crush on me since third grade. And Susan. I'm gunning for her this year."

"Gunning?" Buffy asked, half hoping he didn't mean what she feared he meant.

"Yeah," Cecil said, nodding toward his trophy. "She took fourth place in the spelling bee last year, but this time it's going to be different. I mean, anybody can spell abacus, right?"

"Not in my experience," Buffy replied.

"Sure they can," Cecil said, punching her playfully on the arm. "Abacus. A-b-a-c-u-s. Abacus," he demonstrated. "Want me to use it in a sentence?"

"Please don't," Buffy answered quickly. There was something so . . . she hated to think it, but . . . so *needy* about young Cecil.

"She took fourth in the final round on abacus after I got knocked out by 'awl.'"

"You don't know how to spell 'all'?" Buffy found herself asking in spite of herself.

"Not '*all*'," Cecil corrected her, "'*awl*'."

"Oh," Buffy replied, as if that had cleared it all up for her. As she and Todd had discussed more than once this past week, synonyms had never been her strong suit.

"Still, Bobby cracked like a cheap piggy bank," Cecil went on. "Want to know how I beat him?"

"Okay," Buffy said, absolutely certain that she didn't.

"It was just the six of us. Only five get trophies, so I knew I had to get rid of one of them. Rachel was a lock. Principal Dumbhead Donovan just gave her 'totalitarian' because he likes her. Her mom gives him and all the other teachers cookies at Christmastime.

It's bribery, but what are you going to do? Sun and Ashley are the smartest girls in the whole school. They have the entire *Oxford English Dictionary* memorized. There's no way you're going to beat them. Which left Bobby and Susan. Now I know Susan hates spiders, but I hadn't thought far ahead enough to bring a few spiders in my pocket to shake her. Won't make that mistake again this year, that's for sure. But Bobby . . . he's a sweater. Can't handle the pressure. So just before he goes up for his final-round word, I lean over and whisper in his ear, 'Did you see that?'"

"What?" Buffy asked, jumping to look over her shoulder.

"No, that's what I said to him: 'Did you see that?'" Cecil said, continuing his story.

"Oh, right."

"Then I pointed to the front row where Margaret Johnson was staring up at him. He's had the hots for Margaret since kindergarten. He'd kill for her. But she's always liked Chad. So then I say, 'Margaret just waved at you.' And he says, 'No, she didn't.' And *then* I said, 'Yeah, she did. Better not screw it up now, Bobby.' Then I patted him on the back, like I was his friend, you know . . . like I wanted him to do well, when all I know for sure is that he probably can't spell his name anymore if he thinks Margaret might actually like him. And sure enough, his word is 'circumstance,' and he choked . . . choked . . . choked so hard. . . ."

Cecil slapped his thigh and almost doubled over with laughter. "'Circumstance,'" he began in what Buffy could only assume was an imitation of poor

Bobby Matthews, "'C-e-r,'" Cecil continued, now starting to suffocate on his glee.

"Ding. That was the end of Bobby. You know, it was almost too easy."

"Sounds like it." Buffy nodded.

"Just like when Spiderhead took on the Green Onion. Green Onion's all talking tough and, boom! Spiderhead slashes him right across the throat. Took his head clean off. Want to see?" Cecil said, grabbing the comic book still lying open on his bed.

"That's okay, Cecil," Buffy interrupted, then asked, "Um . . . is anyone else here right now? I mean . . . is your dad home?"

Cecil's face clouded over momentarily. "He's dead," he said simply.

"Oh," Buffy replied immediately. "I'm so sorry."

"Mom said it was a hunting accident, but he'd never gone hunting before that one time and I'm pretty sure a quail can't do that much damage," Cecil said. "Maybe killer quail from the fifth dimension, but I don't—"

"Is your mom home?" Buffy interrupted.

"Sure," Cecil replied, brightening instantly. "Oh . . . it's meat loaf night. Want to stay for meat loaf? My mom makes the best meat loaf in the whole wide world."

"That would be great," Buffy lied.

Cecil inhaled deeply.

"Mmmmm," he almost moaned with delight. "She added lots of extra garlic tonight, I can smell it. Just the way I like it."

"Sounds yummy." Buffy nodded in a manner she hoped was convincing.

"Are your shoes dirty?" Cecil asked, suddenly concerned.

"I don't . . . I don't really think so," Buffy replied, automatically checking the soles of her sneakers.

"My mom won't stand for a dirt trail," Cecil warned. "She works too hard to put up with that kind of nonsense. Maybe you'd better leave your shoes up here with mine. That way, she won't even ask." At this, Cecil crossed to his closet and slid one of the doors open so that Buffy could clearly see, six pairs of adult-Snyder's shoes lined up like good soldiers.

Wait a minute.

There were actually five and a half pairs, Buffy mentally corrected herself. At the far end, right next to the white wingtips, was a single black dress shoe, one of the shoes, if memory served, that Snyder usually wore to school.

"Oh, I'll risk it," Buffy replied.

Suddenly, as Cecil shut the closet door, a singsongy nasal voice shrilled through the air.

"Oh, Cecil . . . time for dinner."

Cecil's face went slack.

"Cecil?" Buffy said. When he didn't respond, she waved a hand in front of his face. "Cecil . . . are you in there?"

Without a word, Cecil walked through the doorway and down the hall toward the stairs.

Buffy glanced around the room once more to make certain there was nothing else about retro-demon dimensions she might need to know. There wasn't. Kneeling, she opened her weapons bag and fished around for the ax. She'd so wanted to try the mace, but this wasn't practice time. Killing demons usually meant beheading, and that was best accomplished with a really sharp slicer. Besides, she had no idea what she'd find when she entered that kitchen.

Buffy rose and took a deep breath to calm herself. The house had been creepy enough. Having what had passed for a civilized discussion with her principal was almost more than her brain could wrap itself around, even if it was a younger version of him.

Okay, she thought.

Time to meet Mommy Dearest.

Chapter Eleven

Buffy made her way gingerly down the staircase and passed through the entry hall, pausing behind the short wall that separated the entry from the dining room. From the sound of clinking dishes still coming from the kitchen, it seemed that both Cecil and his mother had not entered the dining room yet, but Buffy poked her head quickly into the room, just to check. As she'd suspected, it was empty, though there were now two presidential place settings laid out neatly on the table, along with cloth napkins, shiny flatware, and a pitcher of water, already sweating with condensation.

Buffy didn't know exactly why she was so hesitant to face whatever was waiting for her behind that swinging door. Clearly Cecil wasn't going to be any kind of threat to her. Apart from the unsettling possibility that he might ask her to join him for a sleepover, she didn't think there was much he could throw at her in his condition that she couldn't handle.

His mother—well, that was definitely going to be a different story, whether or not she was the demon Buffy'd come through the gateway to kill.

Mothers, whether they were human or demon, shared a willingness to defend their offspring that was particularly dangerous. No matter how often they had butted heads over the years, Buffy had never doubted for a moment that Joyce would willingly have thrown herself in front of a bus for her daughter. Add to that protectiveness demon strength and speed, and you had yourself an enemy that Buffy could not relish facing.

Still, her friends and her own mother were counting on her right now. If she did nothing, or worse, if she failed, Sunnydale would remain under the sleeping spell forever, and those she loved most would never awake. Not an acceptable option.

Shored up by the mental picture of Joyce collapsed on her bathroom floor, Buffy took a deep breath and a firm grip on her ax, and approached the swinging door.

She paused momentarily as the sound of what had to be Cecil's mother's voice grated through the cracks.

"What did you say, young man?"

"I already washed them," Cecil replied evasively.

"Really? You think I can't smell the filth on them?"

The next sound Buffy heard was a muffled *smack, smack,* the sound of an open hand impacting a meaty rear end. A faint *"Ow"* from Cecil confirmed that he'd been on the receiving end. This was followed by water pouring into the kitchen sink and another yelp of pain from Snyder, suggesting that the water was scalding hot, and the whoosh of hands being scrubbed.

"Don't forget to pry that filth from under your nails, young man," the harsh nasal drone added.

"I'm trying, I'm trying," Cecil whined.

"Don't try. Do it."

Buffy felt her ire rising a bit as the scrubbing continued. It was unsettling to hear pain in the voice of a child. Despite his appearance, Cecil was, at least in this place, powerless, and Buffy felt the unusual need to protect him.

Finally, the water was turned off. Buffy pulled back behind the wall and listened as someone entered the dining room and placed several heavy plates on the table. Her stomach started to rumble again at the smell. She couldn't remember the last time she'd had a hot meal. The diet sodas she'd nursed throughout the day didn't count as nourishment. She knew this wasn't the time or the place to indulge in dinner, but she also knew that she was stronger on a full stomach.

The swinging door swished again, and Buffy risked another glance into the dining room. It was, again, empty, but there were now serving plates filled with steaming meat loaf, potatoes, and vegetables in the table's center.

Buffy decided to risk it. She darted toward the table, retrieved a slice of the meat loaf, and took a quick bite.

In an instant, she understood why, despite appearances, this was a demon dimension. Though all the food looked and smelled amazing, it was the foulest thing Buffy had ever put in her mouth. Buffy didn't honestly know what maggots tasted like, but she knew the taste she had imagined whenever she'd seen them crawling over rotting flesh. Suddenly, she needed desperately to vomit, but she took several deep breaths, calming herself, and finally, the wave of nausea passed.

As she collected herself in the entryway, Cecil emerged from the kitchen and took his place at the table. Though he didn't take note of her, Buffy quickly darted across the hall and planted herself behind the corresponding archway that separated the living room from the entryway. From this vantage point she could face the dining room and, by poking her head around the short wall, easily see into the room, but she doubted that whoever or whatever eventually took their place at the head of the table could see her without almost completely turning around.

Her patience was rewarded a moment later as she caught her first glimpse of poor Cecil's mother.

She was not at all what Buffy had imagined, but then, considering the meat loaf, she decided instantly that in this realm, appearances were bound to be deceiving.

Buffy searched her memory for the name of Snyder's mother. She came up with nothing but P names—Patricia, Pamela, Penelope—but none of them sounded right. Finally she settled for Mrs. Snyder.

The woman was a vision of a sweet grandmother in pink flowers and lace. Her white hair was neatly trimmed in a straight bob, and her face was etched with deep lines. The flesh of her neck sagged beneath a generous drooping chin, and her hands, which moved deftly about the table as she served herself and Cecil were veined and covered with age spots. Only her voice betrayed the mettle beneath the deceptively sweet appearance.

Once both of them were served, Mrs. Snyder removed a crisp white apron from around her waist and disappeared briefly into the kitchen to discard it. When she returned, Buffy noted that her shoes were of the orthopedic variety, completing the picture of dowdy, plain, and neat with just a hint of Laura Ashley style.

"How was your day at school?" Mrs. Snyder asked politely as she and her son began to dig into the meal she had placed before them.

Cecil took a generous bite of the meat loaf, and Buffy watched his face for any sign that he would find the dish as disgusting as she had. To her surprise, he ate like a man at his last meal. Her gorge rose as she saw him stuff one forkful after another into his mouth and chew and swallow with great satisfaction.

Buffy thought she'd begun to understand where the torture promised in this dimension might be coming from, but apart from Mrs. Snyder's somewhat overbearing and demanding nature, and perhaps her quickness of temper, Cecil seemed quite happy to be under her care.

"It was great, Mom," Cecil finally answered after a couple of bites.

"Close your mouth, Cecil, until you've swallowed

your food. Haven't I taught you better manners than that?"

Cecil did as he was told, then went on proudly, "I got a B plus on my fractions quiz."

"A B is a B, with or without the plus, young man," Mrs. Snyder answered sharply. "And it certainly isn't an A."

Buffy saw young Cecil's face fall a bit, but he went on gamely. "And I got an A minus on today's spelling quiz."

"An A minus?" Mrs. Snyder asked.

Cecil nodded with a satisfied smile.

"It should have been an A plus," she said dismissively.

"But, you just—" Cecil began.

"I hope you don't think that with grades like that you're going to get anywhere in this life, young man," Mrs. Snyder continued. "An A minus is not an A plus, and you will be an A plus student or you will end up digging ditches like your pathetic excuse for a father. How do you expect to do better than a measly fifth place in this year's spelling bee if you don't even know how to prepare for a test when you're given the words in advance. I am so disappointed in you, Cecil."

"I only missed the bonus words," Cecil tried to defend himself.

"You're weak, Cecil," Mrs. Snyder went on. "You should be ten chapters ahead of everyone else in that class. You're better than all of them, but you refuse to apply yourself. By the time I was your age, I had already been promoted two grade levels above my peers. Your stupidity is unacceptable. You will work harder if I have to stand over you with a belt every minute of the day until your grades improve."

Cecil seemed to have lost his appetite. Buffy could easily understand why. Joyce would have rewarded Buffy warmly for academic performance such as Cecil's. She always wanted Buffy to excel, but never chastised her daughter unless she thought Buffy wasn't doing her personal best. That had always been Joyce's only expectation of Buffy, and to this day, Buffy knew in her heart she had lived up to it, even if her current grades made that hard for Joyce to see.

"You haven't finished your dinner," Mrs. Snyder said with a hint of menace when she noted the same look Buffy had seen on Cecil's face.

"I'm full," Cecil said softly.

Buffy couldn't help the ache that started to pound in her heart at his obvious disappointment. She knew he must have been thinking of his treasured fifth-place spelling bee trophy. She also thought she had begun to understand why he would have gone to such lengths to get it.

"You are an ungrateful worm," Mrs. Snyder replied. "I slaved over that stove for hours today to make your favorite dinner, and this is how you repay my generosity? You will finish every last crumb of food on that plate and you will do it with a smile on your face or so help me this will be the last meal I will ever prepare for you."

Wow.

Finally, Buffy saw clearly the monster she was about to face.

As best as Buffy could tell, Cecil was a pleasant enough child, despite his taste in comic books, and he obviously strove daily to please his mother in everything he did. But there never was nor would there ever be any way of pleasing this woman. People like Mrs. Snyder weren't interested in accomplishment. They were only interested in power.

Buffy had been given a crash course in power once she'd become the Slayer. She'd already learned it was a difficult gift, one she tried to wield with respect and as much humility as she could muster. But Mrs. Snyder didn't understand power. She obviously had needs that little Cecil could never fill, but she would ride him mercilessly in an attempt to force him to do so. She didn't care about Cecil's grades or his dirty hands. She fed off of the power she had over him. She beat him with it, running him down to make herself feel better and to ensure her place of dominance.

It was sick.

And it had undoubtedly made Principal Snyder the man he was.

Buffy had come here imagining all kinds of physical abuse that Snyder might be suffering. Instead, she realized, his punishment at his mother's hands was infinitely more subtle and cruel. By transforming Snyder back into a child and forcing him to submit to her will, the evil demon was ripping apart his heart and tearing at his spirit, just as she had undoubtedly done every day of his young life.

Buffy understood emotional torture. She'd endured it for months at Angelus's hands.

She'd heard more than enough.

Buffy raised the ax that rested in her hand and stepped into the entryway so that both Cecil and Mrs. Snyder could see her clearly. "Hey," she said sharply. "Why don't you pick on someone your own size?"

Mrs. Snyder's face turned quickly. Her mouth hardened into a sneer, and her eyes glinted. "Who are you?" she demanded. "You were not invited to this place and you certainly don't belong here."

"Hi!" Cecil said, smiling at Buffy. "Mom, this is my friend. Can she stay for dinner?"

"Your friend?" Mrs. Snyder said incredulously. "You don't have any friends."

"But, she . . ." Cecil trailed off.

"With the people skills you've taught him, that's almost hard to believe, isn't it?" Buffy interjected.

Mrs. Snyder rose from her seat at the table and moved to face Buffy squarely. "Who are you?" she asked again.

"I'm the Slayer," Buffy said simply. "And you're done. I don't know where you came from and I don't really care. 'Cause you're not going back there either. In fact, I don't think there's a hell hot enough for momsters like you."

"Then you've never seen hell," Mrs. Snyder replied. "But I'll gladly fix that."

Buffy felt her hands start to tingle.

Then she felt the pain as the muscles in her arms and legs began to burn and pull.

Without thought she sent the ax in her hand spinning toward Mrs. Snyder. It embedded itself firmly in her chest with a satisfying thwump, and Buffy instantly felt the pain subside.

"Mommy!" Cecil cried out, rising from the table.

"Stay out of this, Cecil!" both Buffy and Mrs. Snyder shouted in unison.

Cecil replied by rushing to a corner of the dining room, where he cowered in terror, whimpering.

"Probably not a good idea to waste your only weapon so quickly," Mrs. Snyder sneered, pulling the ax from her chest and splintering its handle in her grip. Looking up, Buffy watched as the face of the sweet, beneficent grandmother began to fade. Mrs. Snyder didn't seem bothered by the boils and harsh red welts erupting all over it, spewing pus and yellowish bile. Buffy had to admit, however, that it made what had to come next a little easier. Finally the monster she was fighting looked the part.

"You might want to see a dermatologist about that," Buffy said.

In an instant she closed the space between them and jabbed a quick kick combination into Mrs. Snyder's chest. The demon fell back, crashing into her chair and breaking it to pieces before she hit the floor.

But she was on her feet again, almost before Buffy could recover her balance. Shrieking, she flew at Buffy, her arms outstretched, and grabbed the Slayer by the throat.

Buffy replied with a knuckle punch to the demon's neck. It shocked Mrs. Snyder enough to loosen her grip. Buffy threw both arms up between the demon's, spinning quickly to disengage herself. She completed the turn, crouching low and extending her right leg, and succeeded in taking Mrs. Snyder off her feet.

Once she was down, Buffy landed on top of her and began to pummel her ooze-caked face.

But Mrs. Snyder wasn't going to be finished off that easily. She squirmed for a moment, then, catching one of Buffy's punches in her meaty palm, grabbed Buffy firmly by the waist with her other hand and threw her over her head, sending Buffy flipping through the air and into the china cabinet. Buffy was caught for a moment in a rain of glass shards and splintered wood, but she quickly pulled herself up and, rounding the dining table, caught her breath with the table between them. Mrs. Snyder rose from the ground and began to slowly circle the table toward Buffy.

"Is that all you've got, girl?" Mrs. Snyder demanded.

"Nope. Not even close," Buffy replied.

With that, Buffy leaped up on the table and, grabbing the chandelier above her head, swung herself back for a little momentum before pitching herself feetfirst into the demon.

Mrs. Snyder was thrown back clean through the dining room wall and into the entryway.

She recovered her feet quickly and waited for Buffy to follow. The Slayer did so, landing a series of punishing jabs to her face and torso. Mrs. Snyder answered with a right hook of her own that pushed Buffy back toward the front door.

"You will leave this place!" the demon shouted. "You are not welcome here."

"Oh, don't kid yourself, lady," Buffy replied. "No one is welcome here."

"This is my home!" the demon shouted between punches.

"This isn't a home," Buffy replied with a jump kick that uppercut Mrs. Snyder's jaw. "It's hell."

The insult struck Mrs. Snyder more heavily than any of Buffy's blows.

"You're just a child," Mrs. Snyder replied, sucking wind. "You couldn't possibly understand a mother's love."

"I understand that you don't love your child even a little," Buffy retorted, taking the advantage and knocking the demon to the floor, where she skidded back toward the staircase.

"Cecil is my whole world." Mrs. Snyder shuddered. Buffy couldn't be sure, but she thought that the demon might be on the verge of tears.

"I gave him everything I had to give. I even sacrificed the love of his good-for-nothing father so that Cecil wouldn't be tainted by his bad example."

Buffy paused.

I guess Cecil wasn't wrong about that quail-hunting trip.

Mrs. Snyder pulled herself up and actually seated herself on the bottom stair as she continued. "All I ever wanted was his love."

"I don't believe that for a minute," Buffy replied.

"He was such a timid child."

"Gee, with you as a mother, I can't imagine why," Buffy snapped back.

"As long as he was mine, I could protect him. Push him to do better. Make him see that this world has no place in it for the weak."

"And fun as this little trip down rationalization lane is," Buffy retorted, "could you get up so I can kick your ass some more?"

"He betrayed me," Mrs. Snyder whimpered weakly. Reaching into her pocket, she removed a crumpled piece of parchment, rough around the edges, and tossed it toward Buffy.

Equal parts wary and intrigued, Buffy picked it up and opened it. It was written in a script Buffy didn't recognize, heavy black strokes and curls in an ancient and no doubt evil language. The only words that Buffy could clearly read were midway through the third paragraph: "Paulina Christina Snyder."

Paulina! That's it, Buffy thought, remembering Willow's research.

"You know, my demon-translating skills are kind of rusty," Buffy finally said, tossing the paper back to Paulina.

"He sold me to the demons!" Paulina shrieked with pain and rage. "My own son paid in his flesh and blood to have me banished to a demon dimension!"

Buffy did a little quick math in her head and realized that if Paulina was speaking the truth—and Buffy didn't doubt she was—then Cecil would have made this pact with the forces of darkness well into his adult years.

Paulina had wound herself up into a full rant.

"I gave him my entire life. But that wasn't enough for him. He lived with me for years, even after he'd finished college, and I never said a word. If he was happy here, I was happy to have him."

Maybe we all need to look again at the definition of "happy," Buffy thought.

"And what he gave me in return was an eternal existence in a place . . . I can't begin to describe. No one understands how to make a bed or clean himself properly. They've never even heard of detergent. And the food . . ."

"Picked up a few tips there, did you?" Buffy asked.

Paulina replied with a glare.

"All I wanted was to have my life back to the way it was before Cecil made that terrible mistake. I know if he'd really understood what he was doing, he would never have traded my life so cheaply. I had a little boy who loved me. I just wanted him back here at home, where I could love him and teach him and know that he was mine again. Is that so wrong?"

Buffy couldn't even begin to count the number of wrongs around her. All that she knew for sure was that Paulina Snyder had most certainly reaped what she had sown.

"Look," Buffy said, "I'm not your judge or your jury. The demon dust you use to bring your son back to you every night through that gateway is seeping out into my world and putting everyone to sleep. You want to go back to whatever snake pit you crawled out of, make it quick and don't ever let me see that incredibly ugly face of yours again. Otherwise, it's fight to the death time."

Paulina didn't even take a second to consider Buffy's more than generous offer. Leaping up off the step, she flew at Buffy, punching her hard in the chest and sending her flying back into the dining room.

All right, Buffy thought. *Option two, it is.*

They could trade blows like this indefinitely. Buffy needed to finish this, and for that, she needed a weapon. Her ax lay in pieces on the floor across the room. Though the blade was still intact, it was too far for her to reach with Paulina bearing down on her again. Turning to her left, she found her answer.

The face of President John F. Kennedy.

The image smiled up at her in all of his youthful, charismatic charm. With only a hint of regret, Buffy grabbed the plate, snapped it in half to give herself a sharp edge, and brought it swinging wide across her body as Paulina swooped down upon her. Putting all of her strength into the sweep, Buffy felt the impact of the clean, sharp porcelain blade as it met Paulina's neck, severing her head in one motion.

Paulina's headless body fell across Buffy's. She quickly pulled herself out from beneath it and clambered to her feet, standing to catch her breath amidst the wreckage of the room and the lingering odor of garlic-infused meat loaf that would forever turn her stomach from this point forward.

The first part of her mission accomplished, Buffy started to hurry upstairs to retrieve the trophy and get out when she was stopped in her tracks by the sounds of Cecil whimpering behind her. He still sat in the corner of the dining room, rocking back and forth, his legs pulled to his chest protectively.

"Did you . . . did you see that?" he stammered.

"I had a pretty good seat," she replied.

"Her . . . *face*," he finally forced out.

"Yeah, well, that's what happens when they run out of moisturizer in hell," Buffy said simply.

"No one else has ever seen it," Cecil said, looking up at Buffy in something close to awe. "My friends all think she's so sweet, at least the ones she lets me have over. They don't think much of her cooking, but I guess they just can't handle the spice. Otherwise, though, they think she's a perfect mother. I tried once to tell them about that face, how she changes so quickly when I make her mad, but no one ever believed me."

Buffy paused for a moment, then crossed to Cecil and held a hand out to him. He took it and allowed her to help him to his feet.

"I believe you, Cecil," Buffy said, surprised at the warmth in her voice. "Now, let's get out of here."

Buffy turned to head upstairs, and Cecil was immediately right on her heels. "You're not going to leave me, are you?"

"Nope." Buffy shook her head reassuringly. "I just have to get something. I'll be right back."

Moments later, Buffy was back downstairs with the trophy in her hands. Cecil's face lit up when he saw it.

"Oh, please," he pleaded, "can I have it?"

"Sure," Buffy said. "It's yours, after all." Passing it to him, she took his free hand and together they walked through the gateway and onto the porch.

To Buffy's surprise, it was nearing dawn in Sunnydale. But it was a silent dawn, the same oppressive silence that had hung over Sunnydale the entire day Buffy had waited for Snyder to return to the house for the last time.

Cecil stood on the porch beside her, somewhat disoriented. "What am I doing here?" he asked.

Buffy turned quickly to face him. It wasn't what he said that betrayed him, it was his tone that gave everything away.

"Miss Summers?" Principal Snyder asked incredulously.

There was now no doubt in her mind that little Cecil Snyder was once again buried in the adult Snyder's subconscious, and the man she was facing was going to want an explanation.

She didn't know where to begin.

Fortunately she was spared the need to say anything as Snyder realized he was holding something in his hand. His confused concern gave way to something resembling faint delight as he considered the trophy.

"You know, it's the damnedest thing," he said. "I woke up the other day in my mother's old house, and there it was, just like I remembered it, on my old dresser. I must have been carrying it around with me since then, I just don't remember. . . ." He trailed off.

"My guess is, there will be a lot of that going on," Buffy suggested.

"Where are my shoes?" was Snyder's next question. "Do you know that's the fifth pair of shoes I've misplaced this week?"

Suddenly, Snyder doubled over in pain. At first it seemed that he had been gut-punched, and Buffy instantly went on alert. Invisible demons were rare, but certainly not unheard of, in her experience. Seconds later, however, the source of Snyder's pain became clear. Dropping the trophy, Snyder fell to the porch, both hands grasping his bare left foot. As Buffy watched in fascinated horror, his left pinkie toe was ripped from its rightful place on his foot and disappeared in a magical twinkle of light.

"Owwwww!" Snyder shrieked in pain as blood began to pour from the small gaping wound.

Mystery solved, Buffy thought. *No wonder he's been wearing bloody bandages everywhere he went this week. He must have lost that toe each morning. . . . Oh, wait a minute.*

"Don't tell me," Buffy said, growing queasy at the very idea. "The price you paid in flesh and blood to have your mother banished to a demon dimension was your toe?" she asked in disbelief.

Snyder was in too much pain to answer. He clambered onto all fours, trying to rise up on his remaining good foot.

Buffy started to help him, when another thought occurred to her, a thought that made the oppressive silence around her a little more understandable.

Turning back to the door, Buffy braced herself, then re-entered the house. Sure enough, the gateway was still active and she found herself in the destroyed entry way. Paulina's headless body remained on the floor of the dining room.

It wasn't the trophy at all, Buffy thought. Whatever the demon had stolen was still somewhere in this house and Buffy was going to have to find it to close the gateway and end the spell.

"That's the fifth pair of shoes I've misplaced this week," Snyder had said.

Buffy took the stairs two at a time on her way back to Cecil's room. Hurrying to the closet, she glanced at the five pairs neatly lined on the closet floor and the single black dress shoe that had no mate.

"Poetic, I guess, from Paulina's point of view," Buffy said aloud. Then she grabbed the single shoe and hurried back downstairs and through the front door again.

This time, there was no mistaking her success. Once Buffy had gained the porch, she turned to see the bright light of the gateway swirling behind her as it started to fade. Finally, as the glowing circle grew smaller and smaller, collapsing in on itself, there was an earth-shaking bang, and Buffy found herself staring only at the normal front door.

As if in answer to her unspoken *that had to have worked* thought, Buffy was suddenly aware of the faint chirping of birds and the distant barking of a dog.

Good morning, Sunnydale, Buffy thought with a smile.

She had started down the front walk when she realized she was alone. Snyder was gone, though a fresh trail of his blood told **Buffy he** was limping his way home.

Happy to have avoided any further conversation with the man she could now go back to genuinely disliking, Buffy turned in the opposite direction, grateful that, at last, this much of her work was done and now, like everyone else, she might get a little rest before it was time to face whatever was coming next.

Chapter Twelve

Joyce awakened to find herself in bed and, strangely, in her bathrobe. She couldn't remember much of the night before, but she thought she'd checked Buffy's empty room, realized she was still at the library putting in some extra study hours, *which hopefully would pay off,* and just barely made it into her pajamas before she'd fallen exhausted into bed. She also thought she remembered waking and brushing her teeth, but she decided that must have been one of those early morning dreams where you thought you were getting up and getting dressed to start your day, maybe even were on the way to work, before your alarm started blaring to remind you that you had yet to accomplish any of those things.

It was disorienting and vaguely unsettling, but Joyce tried to shake it off, along with the nagging sense that she could really use another few hours of sleep.

Still, it was clearly the beginning of a beautiful day, and Joyce decided it was best to make a good start of it. Crossing to her bedroom door, she called out, "Buffy?" Though it wouldn't have been the first time Buffy had stayed out all night, Joyce wasn't going to be pleased if her daughter had chosen to spend the evening gallivanting around with her friends rather than getting her rest this close to finals.

"Buffy?" she called again, louder.

Her fears were allayed when she heard from the kitchen below a familiar voice reply, "Mom?"

Joyce barely made it to the staircase landing when Buffy rushed up and threw herself into her mother's arms, hugging her so tightly, Joyce felt her spine popping.

"Good morning, honey," Joyce said warmly once Buffy had released her and she found she could take a full, refreshing breath.

"You're okay," Buffy said with obvious relief, looking her mother up and down in a manner that suggested Buffy was seriously worried that Joyce might have started dating again.

Joyce examined Buffy more closely. Her ponytail was askew, and telltale wisps of hair surrounding her face gave the impression of a good hairdo gone bad. Her denim jacket had a new tear in the right sleeve, and her jeans sported fresh stains that Joyce wanted to believe were dirt or grass but which gave the uncomfortable impression of something stickier.

"Are you just getting home?" Joyce asked, dismayed.

"It was kind of a long night," Buffy replied a little evasively.

"Well, you can tell me all about it on the way to school," Joyce said gamely. She knew Buffy had taken her worries about her studies to heart and Todd's reports to Joyce about Buffy's progress had been promising. Rather then emphasize an understandable lapse, Joyce decided to accentuate the positive and hope for the best. Buffy was a good girl, if a peculiar one, and Joyce knew better than anyone that Buffy was harder on herself than any other critic, including her mother.

"Um, Mom," Buffy said, "it's actually Saturday."

"What?" Joyce asked. She was certain it was Friday.

"Trust me," Buffy said.

Joyce marched back up the stairs behind Buffy and turned on the morning news in her bedroom. Sure enough, she was greeted by the weekend anchors. As she struggled to remember what had happened to Friday, Buffy surprised her by wrapping an arm around her waist.

Joyce responded automatically, draping her own arm over Buffy's shoulder and giving her a firm snuggle.

"Someone's affectionate this morning," she said, smiling.

"I just really love you, Mom," Buffy said simply.

"I love you, too, sweetie," Joyce said, trying to keep the surprise out of her voice. Buffy was sweet, but it had been some time since she'd willingly sought the comfort of her mother's arms. "Are you okay?" she found herself asking.

"Sure," Buffy replied. "I think I'm just appreciating you more than usual right now," she finished.

Oh, God, Joyce thought, and placed the palm of her hand to Buffy's forehead.

"What?" Buffy asked.

"Either you're running a temperature, or you want something," Joyce replied firmly.

Please tell me you didn't burn down the school gymnasium again, Joyce mentally added to the list of things that might be wrong.

"A girl can't just love her mother?" Buffy asked a little defensively.

"A girl can—she just usually doesn't express it this way unless she's brought home a bad test score or found a really cute dress at the mall," Joyce replied.

"Well, this morning, the answer is neither," Buffy said, smiling. "But sometimes I forget how lucky I am to have you as my mom."

"Okay," Joyce said, still at a loss to see where this might be leading.

"You really are something," Buffy finished.

"Where do you think you get it from?" Joyce asked, smiling.

Buffy rewarded her with another squeeze and then started for her room.

"Don't you have another study session this afternoon?" Joyce asked Buffy's back.

Buffy's shoulders slumped visibly. "Oh, that's

right."

"How about some pancakes for breakfast?" Joyce asked. "Get the morning started with some good brain food."

"Since when are pancakes brain food?" Buffy asked.

"Since I didn't make it to the store this week and we're out of eggs and cereal," Joyce answered.

"Sounds perfect," Buffy replied. "Just *after* you've had your coffee, okay?"

Joyce smiled in reply. As her daughter headed toward her bedroom, she sighed, deeply touched by Buffy's uncharacteristic expression of love and happy to take it as a small blessing. She honestly didn't know if she would ever truly understand the little girl she'd brought into the world, but on mornings like this, it hardly mattered.

Buffy was the littlest bit grateful for her evening spent with the Snyders. Though Joyce certainly had her moments, on her worst day she wasn't in the same ballpark, let alone county, as Paulina Snyder. Buffy rarely thought of herself as lucky these days, but the glimpse she'd had into her principal's childhood had been a visceral reminder that there were many people in the world who had it much worse, even if you counted the fact that Buffy had been called to a sacred duty she often wished had been passed to someone else.

As soon as she reached her bedroom she put in a quick call to the library. She spoke to Giles for a few minutes, receiving confirmation that he, Willow, Xander, and Cordelia had all awakened that morning a little worse for the wear, but certainly in good form. Though he attempted to quiz Buffy on the night's events and her encounter with Paulina, Buffy desperately needed a shower and breakfast before Todd showed up, so she deferred his questions to Willow and promised a full debriefing session on Monday morning before class. When Giles asked if she'd had any opportunity to locate Callie, Buffy admitted that she'd seen the whole sleeping spell as the higher priority, and he heartily concurred but insisted that she patrol that evening in search of the young vampire.

Buffy agreed, then called Willow's house to confirm that her best friend had made it home after waking up in the library with Xander and Giles. Willow also wanted a blow-by-blow description of the demon dimension and, given the amount of effort Willow had put into resolving the crisis, Buffy felt honor-bound to satisfy at least some of her curiosity before thanking her profusely and jumping into the shower.

Joyce made good on her pancake threat and, nourished by the delicious and filling breakfast, Buffy decided to forgo her much-needed nap and complete a few of Todd's assignments instead. She was actually feeling quite proud of herself a few hours later when Todd knocked on her bedroom door and she could honestly say she was prepared to work with him.

Todd entered Buffy's room with two tall Styrofoam cups of cold soda already in hand.

"So you're a full-service tutor?" Buffy asked playfully, hoping he would forgive the lack of returned phone calls over the past few days.

His sincere smile and flirty "Let's sit down and define some of those terms" in response put the Slayer immediately at ease.

They were interrupted briefly by Joyce, who poked her head into Buffy's room to announce that she was going to run by the gallery for the afternoon and ask if she could bring home pizza for dinner for all of them. Appropriately embarrassed, Buffy suggested that Todd probably had better things to do, but he seemed to warm to the idea and, with a grateful smile, accepted Joyce's kind offer.

"You've got a great mom," Todd said, once Joyce had left them to work.

"I really do." Buffy nodded, then wondered momentarily if actually liking one's mom would lose her any cool points with Todd. To change the subject, she asked how Todd had been the past few days, apologizing somewhere in the middle for not calling him back sooner.

"Oh, it's no problem," Todd replied quickly. "I actually slept in most of the day yesterday. I don't know what happened. I hope I'm not catching that flu bug that's been going around," he added.

"I'm sure it's nothing a few hours of English history won't cure," Buffy teased as she took a hearty sip of the soda Todd had placed beside her.

"Well, I'm game," Todd replied, searching Buffy's face for something she truly hoped was a sign that she was seriously falling in like with him.

"By the way," Todd continued as he pulled a few reference books out of his backpack, "I haven't seen any sign of the boyfriend you were so worried about."

Buffy felt the tension in her neck and shoulders begin to relax at his words. "I'm glad to hear that," she responded honestly. "He tends to be a night person," she added, hoping to keep Todd on his guard.

Quite suddenly, that sense of relaxation spread down her arms and legs.

Maybe that nap would have been a better idea after all, Buffy thought, worrying that she had finally pushed herself too far.

"Buffy?" Todd asked with genuine concern.

The next thing she knew, Buffy could barely keep her eyes open.

"Buffy?" Todd asked again.

Buffy took a deep breath and tried to reach again for her soda, hoping the caffeine might rejuvenate her somewhat. She fumbled clumsily for the cup and ended up knocking it over onto her desk. Though her instinct told her to jump up and out of the way, she felt positively glued to her chair. To her surprise, Todd also remained where he was, studying her carefully.

"Don't . . . know . . . wha- . . . wrong," Buffy tried to say, but her voice and eyes were beginning to fail her.

The last thing she thought she heard as her world started to spin toward oblivion was Todd saying softly, "I'm so sorry, Buffy."

* * * *

What the bloody hell?

Someone was screaming, someone with a high-pitched piercing wail that Spike could not immediately identify. As the shrieking continued behind him, followed by the distinct sound of the slamming of doors, Spike came fully awake and found himself seated in his wheelchair in Dru's bedroom before the empty four-poster bed.

What was I just doing? Spike wondered. The alarm tightening his gut told him that it was probably important, but clearly not important enough to have stayed awake for.

"Oh, no, you don't, you little brat!" came clearly to Spike's ears.

Angelus.

But Angelus was supposed to be dead.

In a flash, Spike suddenly remembered his last conscious thoughts. Angelus had been sleeping with his beloved Dru, and Callie had carved a small stake that had a date with Angelus's heart.

Spike's unease grew perceptibly as he realized that the stake intended for Angelus now rested with its pointy side embedded deeply in the fabric of his wheelchair, directly between his legs.

"Well, that's rude," Spike muttered aloud before tossing the stake aside and wheeling himself quickly toward the living room.

Once he'd arrived, the story of the last few minutes was painfully clear to him. Angelus and Drusilla stood by the closed French doors. Beyond them, cowering in the few remaining shadows of the patio, which was about to be drenched by full exposure to the morning sun, was Callie, screaming, positively begging to be rescued.

Callie saw Spike before the others did. She started to reach out for him with both arms, calling, "Please, Daddy!" and was rewarded for her efforts by hitting a patch of sun and singeing her arms. She pulled them back instantly but soon cried out for him again.

Spike instinctively moved closer, the whole time figuring the distance to the doors as well as the number of seconds remaining in Callie's afterlife if he didn't do something.

"Don't even think about it, Roller-boy," Angelus said, turning on Spike sharply.

"Oh, I was just moving in for a better view," Spike quipped, hoping his feigned nonchalance would keep Angelus off his guard.

"Callie was a bad, bad girl," Dru offered. "She tried to hurt Angelus."

"I see," Spike said calmly. "While that's most regrettable, don't you think the little bit has learned her lesson?" he asked.

"She's about to," Angelus said menacingly.

He was baiting Spike, and though sorely tempted, Spike refused to rise to it for the moment.

"You know, love," Spike said, turning toward Dru, "she's only a child. *Your* child," he said with emphasis. "Don't you think she deserves a chance to at least explain herself? I mean, Angelus threatened to kill her not two days ago. Maybe she's just . . . acting out?"

"She doesn't love me, Spike," Dru said sadly.

"I tried to make her love me, but she won't."

"In fact, the only one in this house she seems to listen to is you, Spike," Angelus added. "Makes me wonder whose idea it was to crawl into my bed with a stake this morning."

"Oh, don't waste your time, mate," Spike replied. "If I wanted you dead, you'd already be a footnote in history."

Angelus growled, baring his fangs at Spike.

"Now, boys," Drusilla interrupted, "play nice. Callie has come between us all. I think Angelus is right. Things were better before she was here."

Spike didn't know what angered him more, Drusilla or Angelus. Drusilla was insane. He'd always known that and, to a degree, that fact mitigated most of her actions. It was, after all, a good insane, one he'd found incredibly twisted and tempting over the years. But Angelus was playing Dru, pretending to be threatened by Callie because he already knew that Spike had taken a liking to the little girl.

Damn his soulless body to hell.

Spike had options here. His strength had already started to return weeks ago, and for reasons even he was at a loss to delve into too deeply, he had chosen to keep that piece of information from both Angelus and Dru. Still, he was more than capable of rising from his chair and rushing to Callie's rescue, but that would have betrayed his secret. Put simply, Spike had serious "trust" issues with Angelus and he couldn't afford to squander the only advantage he had over him. Dru, he somehow knew, would completely understand and forgive the little deception, should she ever learn of it. In fact, she would probably find it charming. The question was, was Callie worth it?

Spike's heart surprised him for the first time in a long time by saying yes.

Callie continued to cry out to him, her screams growing louder as the sun encroached millimeter by millimeter upon her little corner of life.

Callie was a child, but she was also a good student. Given time and patience, she would become every bit as fierce a companion as Drusilla had been to him. She had already learned to silence what little remained of her conscience, and Spike had delighted in watching her take her first steps into the world of her new vampire existence. It was rewarding in a way he had never before experienced to watch her abandon her old ideas and spark to newer, darker dreams.

Strange as it might seem, Spike had to admit that since Angelus had returned to his and Drusilla's world, Spike had lost something of his love. Dru's attention had been divided at first, but lately, Angelus had been the one she had turned to in most of her needs, and he had gloried in satisfying her, all the while pretending to defer to Spike's intimacy with Dru but clearly only waiting to take Dru from Spike forever.

But Callie was his. She had no love or patience for Angelus and only a little for Dru. Much as Dru said she had wanted this child, the moment Callie had become difficult, Dru had lost interest where Spike had found a project he could literally and figuratively sink his teeth into. Hunting and killing had become new to him, as he experienced them through Callie's eyes, and her uncomplicated love for Spike had soothed the part of his heart so carelessly bruised by Drusilla.

But, were he to defend Callie now, he would be taking sides against Dru and Angelus. Where he had once hoped Callie might be the wedge that would drive Dru and Angelus apart, this would only strengthen their alliance, and Spike might as well pack his bags then and there. Angelus, he could handle. Angelus and Dru united . . . that was a horse of a completely different color.

"It makes no difference to me, love," Spike said, moving closer to Dru and, with pretended carelessness, fondling her hand gently.

Dru shivered appreciatively.

"As long as you're sure that's what you want," Spike added smoothly. "Just last night Callie was telling me what good games you'd been playing at the schoolyard and how much she wanted to find you a new puppy."

"Really?" Dru's face lit up.

Spike shrugged. "But if you think death is an appropriate punishment for teasing Angelus a little, well, you are her mother, so it's entirely up to you."

Dru looked to Spike and then Angelus.

"*Spikey . . . please!*" Callie pleaded through the door, and Spike's head started to pound with fear.

"Perhaps she has learned her lesson, Angelus," Dru said softly.

"Let me make this easy for you, Dru," Angelus replied. "It's her or me. I'm not going to watch my back in my own home."

Dru sighed, resigned.

"Maybe it's for the best," she said.

That was it. Spike had lost. He could still clutch a small victory and spare Callie's life, but it would cost him Drusilla. Angelus would make certain of it.

"As I said, love," Spike replied, "it's your choice."

But the time for choosing was past. Callie's words dissolved into shrieks as the sun finally caught up with her and her tiny body erupted in flames before dissolving into dust.

"I don't know about you, but I'm starving," Angelus said, turning to Drusilla. "I was thinking we might hit the sewers before sundown."

"Sounds lovely," Dru said with a smile. "Care to join us, my darling Spike?"

Spike hesitated to reply. Inside, he was burning, as the image of Callie's death throes etched itself into his memory, adding to the long list of things for which one day he would make Angelus pay.

"That's all right, dearest," Spike finally answered. "I'll just catch up on my programs and find a snack later, a little closer to home."

"Whatever," Angelus said, taking Dru around the waist, pulling her away from Spike. "Maybe we'll bring you back a little dessert."

"Oh, don't put yourself out, mate," Spike replied. "I was never one for sloppy seconds."

Though Spike had appeared to be a vision of complacency over the next half hour as he cooled his rage with a bottle of whiskey and suffered the unbearable torture of pretending to enjoy a golf tournament on television, he was only counting the minutes until Dru and Angelus set off to hunt. He had already decided that he would spend the evening tracking their every move. He'd lost Callie, but he wasn't about to lose Dru as well. He'd keep both eyes on Angelus from this point forward. Soon enough, he'd find a way to separate them forever. Angelus would screw up. Overconfidence such as his always came with a price. Spike just wanted to make sure he had a front-row seat when the bill finally came due.

Chapter Thirteen

When Buffy awoke, her head pounding, limbs heavy with fatigue and mind still shrouded in a hazy mist, the first thing she was conscious of was the fact that she was lying on her bed. The room was dark, though not quite pitch black. If she'd had to guess, she would have called it dusk outside.

She tried to sit up, but an anvil seemed to be sitting atop her shoulders. The best she could manage initially was to rise up on her elbows and scan her bedroom.

What the hell happened? kept running through her mind like a song that was stuck and stubbornly refused to go away.

A sharp gut-punch of memory brought her more fully to her senses when she made out the figure of Todd standing in the shadows near her bedroom window. His arms were crossed, but he leaned against the wall in what looked like relative comfort.

"Buffy?" he said. There was hope in his voice. But there was also something else: sadness, maybe . . . tinged with a bit of fear.

"What the hell happened?" Buffy finally said, giving voice to the most coherent thought in her head.

Todd didn't answer her directly at first.

"My guess is that you're still a little hazy from the tranquilizers I put in your soda. I didn't ask, but I think they're commonly used on elephants. The man who sent them to me swore you wouldn't be hurt by them, just weakened."

Todd was right. Buffy was still hazy. But she was also growing more and more alert each second. She had no idea now who or what Todd really was, so to lull him further into a false sense of security, she remained where she was and intentionally paused longer than necessary between her words, hoping Todd would still assume she was not a serious threat to him.

"You gave me . . . elephant . . . pills?" she asked. "Why?"

His answer struck Buffy directly in the gut more forcefully than a perfectly timed punch.

"I was hired to kill you," Todd said simply.

The haze in Buffy's mind vanished completely. Though Todd still stood across the room from her, he straightened his posture and moved into the only light available, cast by Buffy's desk lamp. She still couldn't see his face clearly, but she recognized the relaxed demeanor of a foe who honestly believed he was in charge of the situation.

Well, you're just King Wrong from Wrongville, Buffy thought as every muscle in her body tensed and she struggled to resist the urge to fly across the small space that separated them and pin him to the floor before pounding the answer out of him she now required.

"You change your mind, or do you get paid by the hour?" Buffy asked wryly.

Todd took a hesitant step closer to the bed.

"I can't do it, Buffy," he said, almost desperately.

You sure as hell can't now, Buffy thought.

Buffy pulled herself up to a sitting position, taking much more time than she needed, and noted that Todd quickly stepped back again. His nerves were definitely starting to show.

"Okay." She sighed. "Why don't you start somewhere closer to the beginning?"

Todd nodded, then started to pace slowly as he spoke.

"A man contacted me. He offered me a full ride to U.C.-Sunnydale and any graduate program in the country in exchange for my cooperation. He knew you were on the list for special tutoring and he said he could make sure I was assigned to you." Todd paused, swallowing hard before he went on. "He said you were a killer, a vicious killer."

"He" wasn't necessarily wrong.

"He said you were a danger to Sunnydale, but that you'd never be prosecuted for your crimes. He sent me your record and frankly, it wasn't hard to believe him. Vandalism, arson, assault—it's all there in black and white."

"Weren't you the one who told me that history was written by the victors, so it's not always a good idea to believe everything you read?" Buffy asked.

"I was," Todd agreed, "and I didn't, especially after we met. It just didn't seem possible. But, then . . ." he trailed off.

"Who was he? Who hired you?" Buffy asked softly.

"He never gave me a name."

We'll see about that.

"Okay, then what?" Buffy demanded, more sternly than she'd intended.

"I saw you at the park night before last. You were fighting two grown men. I couldn't see everything, but I saw you fight. You were stronger than they were. And you were the only one who walked away from that fight," Todd said, obviously struggling with his own confusion.

"I'd already tried to tell him I couldn't do it," he went on. "But after I saw that, I decided I had to. I came here today, so certain of what I had to do. But once you were asleep, I just couldn't."

"Why not?" Buffy asked, going for alluring and pretty sure she already knew the answer.

"I didn't expect to like you so much, Buffy," he said sadly.

Buffy figured those were pretty much the high points of Todd's story and she wasn't in the mood to coax anything further from him.

In the space of a breath she was off the bed and a startled Todd was pinned against the wall, Buffy's arm pressing firmly on his chest and his options now severely limited.

"Why don't you just ask me what you've been wanting to ask me all day, Todd?" she said firmly. "This has nothing to do with liking me. This is about satisfying your curiosity, isn't it?" she demanded. "Ask me, Todd."

Todd had broken out in a cold sweat the moment he was pinned. It was clear that he now realized he had misjudged Buffy in more ways than one, and struggled to find the answer that would satisfy her. As it happened, it was also the only true question he'd had from the moment they met.

"Who . . . what are you?" he stammered.

Buffy smiled.

"I'm the thing the darkness fears," she replied.

Forcing her arm harder into Todd's chest, she asked, "Who hired you?"

"I told you, I don't know," he said, clearly distressed.

"I heard what you said," Buffy replied. "I just don't believe you."

"I swear to God," Todd insisted. "The guy never used his name. He just promised half the payment up front, and when I contacted the registrar's office, they confirmed that my school account had been paid up through next year."

"I saw you on the phone, Todd," Buffy said simply. "I heard you talking to someone. You at least have a phone number, don't you?"

Todd shook his head. "That call was prearranged. I

just had to wait by the phone at a certain time, I swear."

Buffy searched his terrified face. He was scared, but he was also telling the truth. Abruptly, she lowered her arm and stepped back. For a moment, Todd looked like exactly what he was: a condemned man who had just been offered a last-second reprieve.

"You have no idea how lucky you are," she said as he caught his breath. "See, everything you think you know about me is true . . . from a certain point of view. You don't deserve the truth, Todd, not after the way you've lied to me and put my life in danger, but I will tell you this much: I do fight. I fight evil. The man or whatever the hell hired you undoubtedly fights too, just for the wrong team. You did the right thing here today. And my guess is, you're going to pay for it with your life. Oh, I'm not going to hurt you," she went on in response to the genuine terror that flashed across his face. "That's not my job. Times like this, I wish it was, but it isn't. I'm going to leave you to him, and believe me when I tell you, men like that don't tolerate mistakes."

Todd considered her carefully. He must have seen more clearly than ever before how complicated the young woman standing before him was. Buffy felt his regret, but it didn't console her one bit.

"I'm so sorry, Buffy," Todd said honestly.

"Yeah, I heard that the first time you said it," Buffy tossed back. "Now get out."

Todd did as he was told, without bothering to collect his bag or books.

Torn between rage and confusion, Buffy listened

for the slamming front door, then watched from her bedroom window as he hurried down her front walk.

Once she was satisfied he was gone, she turned from the window and threw herself back down on her bed.

If I had a nickel for every guy who ever fell in love with me and then tried to kill me . . . , she thought sadly.

You'd have a dime, a more rational voice inside her head offered. *Twenty cents at the most.*

After leaving Drusilla to her fun in the alley behind the movie theater, Angelus had hurried to Buffy's house just after sundown. Though he couldn't help but feel he'd lost some momentum over the past few days, he sincerely hoped that Buffy and Todd hadn't. After mulling over his options, he'd decided the most elegant approach was usually a simple one. He didn't honestly believe that Buffy was nearly as close to Todd as she'd suggested, but there was an easy enough way to find out. The next time Buffy and Todd met, Angelus intended to be there, and assuming the time was ripe, he would slowly torture Todd before Buffy's eyes.

At least, that had been the plan. And, initially, it had looked promising.

When Angelus arrived at Buffy's window, he'd seen Buffy sitting up in her bed talking with Todd. Their voices had been pitched too low for him to make out all of their conversation, but he certainly caught the significant points of interest.

Turned out there really was more to Todd than met

the eye. Angelus had seen Buffy's determination and strength. He'd smelled Todd's fear. And he'd witnessed the sadness written plainly on Buffy's face once Todd was gone. It wasn't exactly the epic despair he'd hoped to create that night, but it would do.

Thing was, it was also the slightest bit irritating. Todd's death now wouldn't hurt Buffy nearly as much as Angelus had hoped. She might even be expecting it, though not necessarily at Angelus's hands. And if Todd had any sense, he'd be on his way right now to have some eyes installed in the back of his head. But Buffy was Angelus's special project. He struggled with the disquieting sense that someone had invaded his territory.

At least the solution was uncomplicated.

One moment, Todd was hurrying down Ravello Drive toward the center of town, and the next, he'd been plucked from the sidewalk by the back of his shirt collar and deposited on the ground pinned down by Angelus's foot in his gut.

"You hurt Buffy," Angelus said menacingly.

He saw something like recognition along with the terror in Todd's eyes and could only assume that Buffy had mentioned something about him to Todd.

Good to know my reputation is still intact, he mused.

"I . . . I . . . don't," Todd was trying to find words.

"Shhh," Angelus hissed softly as he lifted Todd from the ground and held him firmly by the throat. "No one gets to do that but me," he whispered.

Bringing Todd's neck to his lips, Angelus sunk his

teeth into the traumatized tutor and within moments had sucked every last drop of life from him.

"Is that the nasty teacher man?" a dulcet voice sung in his ear as he was reveling in the intense pleasure of a fresh kill.

Angelus dropped Todd to the sidewalk and turned to face Drusilla, noting that her own mouth was still wet with the blood of her most recent feeding.

"It was," Angelus replied with satisfaction.

"But where's Buffy?" Dru asked. "I thought you wanted her to see this."

"Slight change of plans, dearest," Angelus said, drawing Dru close with one arm and firmly pressing her lithe frame into his.

"That's my Angelus," Dru cooed. "One never knows what he'll do next."

"You always know," Angelus said suggestively, and punctuated the remark by planting a firm kiss on Dru's mouth. He tingled with pleasure as she licked the last of Todd from his lips.

"Promise me . . . ," she whispered as they pulled apart.

"Anything," Angelus replied.

"Promise me that in the days to come, the whole world will bleed."

"That's definitely the idea," he assured her.

Dru clapped her hands in delight, then draped her arm across Angelus's shoulders as they strolled up the street.

"The stars and the moon," she sang softly.

"So tell me, my sweet," Angelus interrupted her. "Who would you like for dessert?

Spike stepped into the light of a streetlamp just outside Buffy's house and watched as Angelus and Dru meandered, oblivious to his presence. Though he believed he should have been feeling something like simmering rage at the sight, he found the experience strangely cold. What he had just witnessed was what he had always imagined when Dru and Angelus set out into the night together. Confirmation of his fears did nothing but steel his resolve.

The more unexpected part of the experience was the detachment that washed over him as he watched Dru snuggle into Angelus's arms.

After a moment, he dropped his gaze to Todd's body. He couldn't manage to feel anything at all. It had nothing to do with his timeless love for Drusilla. That feeling lived in a part of his heart to which no one else would ever be granted access, and it wasn't going anywhere anytime soon. But something else had clicked into place, and Spike examined it from a palpable distance.

It definitely had something to do with Callie. Forced to hide the genuine regret he felt at her death, he'd simply done his best to refuse to let those feelings surface within him. Those feelings were best left alone. They drove a person to do incredibly insane things; things almost as insane as most of Angelus's actions of late.

So what's his excuse? he wondered.

Angelus was allowing his obsession with the Slayer to blind him to a very obvious reality.

He's not hurting her at all. He's just pissing her the hell off. And a pissed-off Slayer is one thing none of us needs right now.

Suddenly, something else was quite clear to Spike. It was just a thought. But it was an incredibly intriguing thought.

Spike had made his fair share of enemies over the years. It came with being the big bad. And the Slayer had, for more than a year now, definitely been near the top of his list of those who would undoubtedly be better off dead.

Funny thing about enemies, though, and the company they keep. The only thing Spike hated more than the Slayer right now was Angelus. And Angelus was undoubtedly the thing that the Slayer hated most of all.

Ergo . . .

The enemy of my enemy might just be my friend.

Spike allowed the thought to wind its way through his mind, a faint flicker of delight growing brighter as it coursed through him.

That flicker was only extinguished when the Slayer knocked him to the ground and began her assault to his face with her fists.

Buffy had grown restless, sitting in her bedroom, thinking about Todd, and imagining what might have been if just once, a cute boy with a quick wit and a sparkling personality turned out to be no more than that.

The only sure-fire way Buffy knew to deal with the regret was to stop dealing with it. And the best way to do that was to focus her attention on something else. Something she could do something about with a stake or a crossbow.

She had already planned to find Callie that evening. Though her mother would be home soon with pizza for three, Buffy soon found herself scratching out a quick note expressing her sincere desire for leftovers, and heading out into the darkness to do the one job she knew she did well.

And then she'd seen Spike.

Standing over Todd's very dead body.

It's amazing how the universe works, Buffy thought as she tackled him from behind. It had taken Todd from her, even before Spike had made a meal out of him, but it had also given her exactly what she needed in order to find Callie . . . the only person in town besides Buffy who had definitely seen her in the past few days.

It probably wasn't a fair trade, especially from Todd's point of view, but she'd take it.

Buffy had fought Spike several times in the past. He was incredibly strong and equally quick, but that wasn't what made him so dangerous. Though it was always tempting to dismiss the bad Billy Idol wannabe fashion sense, Spike was easily the most tenacious vampire she'd ever faced. The guy just didn't know the meaning of the word "quit," and he seemed to truly enjoy pain, both the giving and the receiving.

So she had a hard time understanding what the hell

his problem was at the moment. He'd just made a fresh kill. He should have been brimming over with fight. But instead of tossing her off and laying into her with all his might, he was dodging her punches without throwing any of his own.

Come to think of it, this is the first time I've seen him out of his wheelchair, Buffy realized. *Maybe he's not quite up to strength.*

Finally, Buffy's curiosity got the better of her. She didn't stop punching, but she did ask, "Is it me, or is your heart just not in this?"

"If you'd just stop for a minute, I might answer that," Spike replied between blows.

In a quick motion, Buffy grabbed Spike by his collar and rolled to her right. She then picked him up and forced him off balance, tossing him into a nearby tree. She pulled back, expecting a charge, but Spike surprised her again by slowly rising to his feet and holding up his hands in the universal sign of "I surrender."

"Okay," Buffy said, "you want to play nice. Tell me one thing. Where can I find Callie McKay?"

"She's dead," Spike said with obvious, and what seemed like genuine, regret.

Buffy didn't want to believe him, but she couldn't help herself. She did.

"Angelus killed her," Spike went on with a hint of anger.

Buffy was stunned. On the one hand, she was definitely relieved. She hadn't honestly been looking forward to solving this problem, but she'd known what she had to do and was prepared to do it. On the other hand, *why should this bother someone like Spike?*

"Did Angelus sire her in the first place?" Buffy demanded.

"No, that was Drusilla," Spike replied. "She wanted a new toy and then got bored when it didn't dance to her tune."

Buffy could hardly believe what she was hearing.

"Callie was a good kid." Spike shrugged. "But she didn't fancy Angelus, and he, being the bigger and badder of the two, made quick work of her."

"Boy, you guys are really something," Buffy said.

"You don't know the half of it, pet," Spike replied almost cordially. "Oh, and P.S., he's also the one who killed your little friend there. Not that I mind taking credit for a good kill, but that was Angelus's doing."

The nonchalance with which Spike tossed this out galled Buffy. After Todd's confession, she wouldn't have put good money on him surviving the week. Whoever had hired him to kill a Slayer must have been playing in the big leagues of evil. The fact that Angel had gotten to him first was really just a matter of being in the right place at the right time. She couldn't help but wonder, however, why he hadn't made more of a show of it for her benefit.

Maybe he knew the truth about Todd before I did and he was just clearing his own way, she decided.

Either way, this was no time to get too wound up in the mystery. She was, after all, still facing the only vampire she'd ever confronted who had actually killed a Slayer. Two, if memory served.

"So what's your story?" Buffy asked. "You just out for a walk?"

"Honestly, I've been thinking," Spike surprised her by saying.

"Not your strong suit, Spike," Buffy replied.

"Hear me out," he said. "I know you want to off Angelus, but up until now, you've played right into his hands. You want to beat him, you have to stop playing defense. Take the bloody fight to him."

"And you're telling me this why?" Buffy asked.

"I don't know. I'm a puzzle, aren't I?" Then Spike almost smiled, shook his head, and took off running down the street.

Buffy found herself strangely reluctant to follow, so stunned was she by both the message and the messenger. It only took her a moment to come to a shocking revelation.

He's right.

She hated to admit it, but he was. For weeks she and Giles and the rest of her friends had driven themselves crazy researching Angelus's past and trying to foresee his next move. She knew their final confrontation was just around the corner, and she'd busied herself preparing to face him whenever and however he eventually chose to come after her. In fact, the only one of them who had taken any kind of offensive action against Angel had been Giles, and only when he was in a blind rage over the death of Jenny Calendar. Though Buffy had chastised Giles for rushing in, he had succeeded in destroying the factory that Angel, Dru, and Spike had called home. Only Giles had scored anything resembling a point in their favor recently.

So what the hell was she waiting for?

The deaths of Callie and Todd would trouble Buffy's dreams in the coming days. But infinitely more troubling would be Spike's advice. It would force her to ask again and again the question she'd been avoiding and to see clearly the answer she'd only thought she had come to accept.

Buffy had been waiting. Subconsciously. Unintentionally. Whatever. She'd been biding her time, telling herself that she was preparing for the coming battle, but in reality, she had been waiting for some kind of miracle that would make the nightmare end and bring Angel back to her.

But Angel wasn't coming back. The time for hopes and dreams had past.

Buffy now knew what she had to do.

She would only lose sleep now wondering why Spike had been the one to make her see it.

Chapter Fourteen

Monday morning, about half an hour before class was to begin, Buffy and Willow were on their way to the library to check in with Giles. Everyone including the Slayer had done much catching up on lost sleep over the weekend and as best Buffy could tell, things were back to as normal as they ever got on the Hellmouth.

"I'm really sorry to hear about Todd," Willow said once she'd gotten the whole sordid story from Buffy.

"Which part?" Buffy asked.

"I guess the 'he was really trying to kill you' part," Willow decided, "though I'm also not happy that Angel killed him." After a moment, she added, "You don't think Angel . . . you know . . ."

"Turned him?" Buffy finished the sentence for her. "The funeral was yesterday," Buffy replied. "I didn't attend, but I did spend some time there last night making sure Todd wasn't just *mostly* dead."

"Well, that was almost thoughtful of Angel," Willow suggested.

"No brownie points on this one, Wil," Buffy said decisively. "Angel is evil. And he's going to go the way of all evil that is unfortunate enough to cross the Sunnydale city line."

"What did your mom say about Todd?" Willow asked, as much to derail the Angel conversation as anything.

"I told her he wouldn't be coming back. She wasn't pleased about it until I told her it was because he'd developed sort of a crush on me and I didn't think that was appropriate in a student-tutor relationship," Buffy replied.

"Well, it was sort of true," Willow said.

"It was as much of the truth as she needs to know," Buffy agreed. "I think she was actually a little impressed that I showed so much emotional maturity, given the circumstances. She said that as long as my grades stay up through finals, she won't insist on hiring another tutor anytime soon."

Willow paused thoughtfully. "You know you've got a great mom, don't you?"

"I do." Buffy nodded.

"Come to think of it, I wouldn't mind trading," Willow added.

"Is Mrs. Rosenberg still restriction-happy?" Buffy asked.

"She's mellowed a bit. No more afternoon curfew.

But she's still looking into that kibbutz," Willow said with disappointment.

"Don't worry," Buffy said reassuringly. "There's always a chance the world will end before you have to go."

"Very true." Willow nodded. "Or maybe she'll just conveniently forget. It wouldn't be the first time."

"Good morning, Buffy, Willow," Giles said cheerfully as they entered the library. Xander and Cordelia were there as well, seated side by side on top of the main table, clearly awaiting the arrival of the Slayer.

"So, Buffy," Xander said enthusiastically, "you saved the world . . . again. What are you going to do now?"

"I'm going to see how I did on my latest chem quiz, and turn in a truly spectacular essay on Victorian poetry," Buffy replied without missing a beat.

"I must say, Buffy, you really did a wonderful job this past week," Giles said.

"Thanks," Buffy replied. "A few more like this and I should make employee of the month in no time."

"Yes, we'll see about getting you a plaque," Giles joked.

"Or a good set of steak knives," Xander suggested. "Or maybe just a really good set of stakes. You know, not the everyday stakes, but the kind you only bring out on special occasions."

As everyone had spent their waking weekend hours trading telephone accounts of Buffy's adventures with the principal as well as the secret identity of her tutor, there was little else to discuss at this point, and the group seemed pleased to default to attempts at witty banter.

"I do have a question for you, Buffy," Giles interjected.

"Shoot, Coach."

Giles accepted her retort as gracefully as possible before asking, "Did you happen to know a freshman by the name of Joshua Grodin?"

Buffy thought before replying. "Doesn't ring any bells."

"I have him in my fourth-period computer lab," Willow offered. "Why?"

"He's dead," Giles said seriously.

"Oh, no." Willow sighed. "He was a really good student. Kind of quiet. I think his mom died last year."

"Yes, well, his body and that of his father were found dismembered in their basement last week. Apparently the neighbors started to complain about the smell. The police contacted me because they found this book among his things," Giles went on, passing the old, leather-bound tome to Buffy for her perusal.

"*Raising Demons*?" Buffy asked as she read the title.

"It's from my private collection," Giles said somberly.

"He keeps it right next to his first edition of *Demon Recipes: One Hundred Ways to Eat Entrails*," Xander offered.

"Did Joshua steal it?" Buffy asked Giles.

"He must have." Giles nodded. "And he appears to have paid quite a high price for it."

"So that's how Paulina got into Sunnydale?" Willow asked.

"It's hard to know for sure," Giles replied. "None of the spells in the book relate specifically to her, but she was a relatively new demon and might have been able to answer Joshua's call. At any rate, it's highly likely that the two events were connected."

"Well, I think we can all learn a valuable lesson from this," Cordelia interjected.

"What's that?" Buffy asked.

"Raising demons is bad," she said as if it weren't already obvious.

"And they say kids aren't learning anything in school these days," Xander quipped. "It's not all about test scores, you know."

Buffy wanted to let it go, but she had come to the library that morning with a purpose, and taking Giles aside, she asked quietly, "Have you had a chance to find out anything about the person or persons who might have hired Todd?"

Giles shook his head. "It's hardly the first assassination attempt, Buffy, nor is it likely to be the last. Though for a demon to hire a human, it's just . . ."

"What?" Buffy asked.

"Pedestrian," Giles replied. "Normally any self-respecting demon would look to the Order of Tiracca, or the Benevolent Brotherhood of Malpasa . . ."

"The Benevolent Brotherhood . . . isn't that kind of false advertising?"

"At any rate, Buffy, you must remain on guard," Giles warned her.

"I am. And I will. But I think we should talk more later about Angel."

"Why is that? You said yourself you don't think he was responsible for hiring Todd."

"I think we might want to consider some new tactics," Buffy countered. She hadn't gone into detail yet with Giles about her encounter with Spike, apart from reporting his news about Callie. But she hadn't been able to stop thinking about it either. "It might be time to start playing offense instead of defense," she added.

"It's definitely worth considering." Giles nodded. "See you after classes?"

"Where else would I be?" Buffy asked, then added, "Isn't that depressing?"

"Hey, Buffy," Xander interrupted from across the room, "tell me again about the toe."

"The toe?" Giles asked. "Do I want to know?"

"Xander, we've been over this," Willow said, obviously not warming to the topic.

"No, I mean, did it just disappear, or was there actual ripping involved?" Xander wanted to know.

"There was ripping," Buffy nodded. "And then there was lots of blood."

"It *is* actually kind of fascinating that Principal Snyder regrew that toe every night when he entered the demon dimension," Willow said.

"Paulina said she wanted her son back just the way he was when he was a little boy," Buffy reminded them. "I guess that included toes."

"I wonder what's worse," Willow said, "losing that toe every morning when he left the gateway, or living with the idea that he sold it in the first place to get rid of his mother?"

"Personally, I want to know who in the demon world is so toe-happy that they'd accept Snyder's littlest piggie as payment in full for turning someone into a demon," Xander added.

"Did anyone see the game this weekend?" Cordelia interrupted, apropos of nothing.

"What game?" Xander asked.

"I don't know. It was the weekend. Somebody must have played somebody else at something. I'm just done with all this talk about ripping and toes," Cordelia replied.

Xander jumped off the table and helped Cordelia to her feet as well. "And that's our cue, ladies and gentleman. Time for another fun-filled day at Sunnydale High."

"See you guys at lunch?" Buffy asked as they made their way into the hall.

"Absolutely," Xander replied. "Fish sticks all around, on me."

Willow and Buffy exchanged a smile at Xander's generosity as they passed the principal's office and the group went their separate ways toward their respective classes. Though Snyder's office was unoccupied, Buffy did pause long enough to note through the office door window that the spelling bee trophy that had been retrieved from Paulina's home now sat on one corner of Snyder's bookshelf. It wasn't exactly a place of honor reminiscent of the dresser top, but it would also never be out of Snyder's eye line when he was seated at his desk, Buffy realized, surprised by the twinge of sadness that welled up inside her at the sight.

In all of the telling and retelling of the story of her encounter to her friends and her Watcher, Buffy had found herself leaving out the details about the spelling bee and the trophy. She didn't know why. It wasn't embarrassing for her in any way. She just felt strange about it. It was like seeing somebody's report card or test score by mistake. Snyder and his love for that trophy, despite the tactics he had used in order to acquire it, was somehow too private for casual conversation. It was like she'd seen him naked, and that was a memory she was determined to bury as soon as humanly possible.

Still, as she passed him a few doors down in the hall berating a freshman girl publicly for the length of her miniskirt and the height of her shoe heels, Buffy found the unpleasant memory easier to bear.

It takes a monster to make a monster, Buffy thought to herself as she passed him, pleased that he hadn't even bothered to glance in her direction.

"Isn't that right, Cecil," she said just soft enough that he might not have heard it.

Buffy would never know if he had, but she would often wonder. The moment the words left her mouth, Snyder stopped his harangue in mid-sentence, looked quickly around the hall and, with a huff, hurried back toward his office.

Buffy smiled to herself as she saw the immediate relief on the young student's face at her sudden reprieve. Being the Slayer was a huge responsibility. But from time to time, it also came with unexpected rewards.

Epilogue

Monday was Mayor Richard Wilkens's favorite day of the week. And Monday morning was the best time of his favorite day. The offices of city hall positively buzzed with activity and energy. His staff reported for work, well rested from their weekend, optimistic and ready to face the week's challenges. It was truly the time when all seemed most possible.

This particular Monday was especially gratifying as many of his staff members had been out of the office sick toward the end of the previous week. The mayor himself had only worked a half day on Thursday before heading home with what felt like a bad case of the flu and remaining in bed until Saturday morning. But the mayor was pleased to see that everyone was attacking their work on this beautiful Monday morning with both gusto and verve.

There was a knock on his office door so slight that he almost missed it what with closing and refolding the comics section of the morning newspaper.

That Allan, always so cautious, the mayor thought to himself. He had often wondered whether or not that was really a good thing. Deference and respect were important. But so was confidence. He made a mental note to recommend Allan for an upcoming Dale Carnegie Leadership Seminar. It would do the young man good.

"Come in," Mayor Wilkens said pleasantly. Allan entered the office carrying a number of file folders, undoubtedly for the mayor's review. He looked as if whatever he had eaten for breakfast that morning had not agreed with him.

"Good morning, sir," Allan said quietly. It was like he knew he had to say it but at the same time wished he could express the sentiment and not be in the same room with his boss.

"Good morning," the mayor replied with a smile. "I'm no psychic, Allan, but I don't think I need to be one to see those dark stormclouds hanging over your head this morning."

The mayor rose from the chair behind his desk and caught the brief flinch Allan made before retreating as casually as he could back toward the office door, still clutching his file folders.

Undeterred, the mayor continued the short walk around to the front of his desk, where he then perched himself and crossed his arms.

"I know. It's no fun taking your medicine, but best

to just swallow it down and move on. What's the bad news, Allan?" he asked evenly. "What could possibly spoil such a beautiful spring day?"

Allan swallowed hard. "Sir, it's Todd Harter."

The mayor's eyes darted to Allan's. He held his assistant's gaze for a moment, just long enough to be certain that the rest of that sentence was not going to have a happy ending.

"Go on," the mayor said gamely.

"He . . . he . . . he's dead, sir," Allan finally finished. The mayor sat for a moment as Allan studied his face, no doubt anticipating the disappointment with which the mayor would greet this news.

The mayor rose from his desk, paced a few times to and fro before it, then paused to say, "Well, that's a darn shame."

Allan's relief was so obvious, the mayor almost thought he might burst into song right then and there.

Come to think of it, there are ways to make that happen, the mayor mused. *Could be fun for a while.*

"Cause of death?" the mayor asked, getting back on track.

"Um, severe"—Allan paused, searching for the right word—"anemia," he replied.

"I see," the mayor said sadly, then added, "He was such a bright young man, and with a promising future ahead of him."

"I have assembled a list of other potential candidates for the position, sir," Allan added quickly. He then approached the mayor, holding out his precious file folders.

The mayor nodded appreciatively. "Leave them on the desk. I'll review them later this afternoon," he said. He was pleased to note that Allan had labeled the folders "Candidate 1," "Candidate 2," etc., rather than "Potential Slayer Assassins," and for that he was grateful. Discretion was a difficult quality to come by in assistants at Allan's level, and the young man was proving that he possessed that in abundance.

"Anything else?" the mayor asked as Allan turned toward the door.

"Not at the moment, sir," Allan replied.

"Very good."

Allan had almost made it out when the mayor added, "Oh, Allan?"

The young man turned back, as if he knew he had escaped too easily. "Yes, sir?"

"Did I hear that one of our local vampires decided to turn a child last week?"

"Uh, I believe so, yes." Allan nodded.

"Am I wrong, or is that just not done?" the mayor asked.

"It is . . . unusual, sir," Allan replied, choosing his words extremely carefully.

"Check into it for me, will you?" the mayor asked pleasantly. "Can't have the demon population running completely amok on my watch, can we?"

"No, sir."

"Excellent." The mayor nodded. "Carry on."

"Thank you, sir," Allan said, then hurried from the office, closing the door quietly behind him.

Once he was alone again, the mayor stood for a

moment before his desk, considering the file folders. Though he was certain that Allan had assembled a strong list for him, he doubted that the right person combined with the right opportunity was anywhere among them. Slayers were both a blessing and a curse, in the mayor's experience. On the one hand, they did keep the vampire population under something resembling control. That was good for the city and, therefore, good for city hall. On the other hand, they were a powerful force for good. The mayor didn't mind that, in theory. But as he had carefully laid out his time line for the next twelve months, it had occurred to him that things would be considerably less complicated for him if Sunnydale's Slayer were to meet her end well before next May, and the next Slayer to be activated come from a place very far from Southern California.

It was a nice thought. Long-range strategic planning was one of the mayor's strong suits, after all. But it was doubtful that he was going to find another human being with Todd's advantages, the ability to get close to the Slayer for a plausible reason and then betray her when she was at her weakest. If memory served, the Slayer's eighteenth birthday would be coming up in a few months and her cruciamentum, her rite of passage trial of strength, might provide another such opportunity, but whatever the mayor chose to do, he would have to play it very carefully. Above all, he must remain as far from suspicion as it was possible to get until the last hundred days before his Ascension.

And who knew? Maybe Buffy Summers would find a way to get herself killed well before then with or without his interference. Slayers weren't known for their longevity. It was an unfortunate occupational hazard. At least the second Slayer, Kendra, who had only come to the mayor's attention a few weeks earlier, lived very far from Sunnydale. With a little luck, they might never cross paths.

Despite Allan's efforts, the mayor decided that the files he'd brought him that morning were best kept out of sight. He collected them and crossed to the wall opposite his desk, which was hung with some of the many commendations and certificates he'd received over his many years of public service in Sunnydale. Reaching for a recessed button in the wall, he opened a hidden compartment that displayed memorabilia and commendations of a very different order, though also a memorial of sorts to the many services he had provided to the city in his several hundred years as a resident.

A number of personal files were kept in this cabinet, along with an impressive display of ceremonial swords, daggers, a few potions too dangerous to leave out, and the odd ancient artifact. One such artifact caught his attention as he placed the file folders in a secret drawer: a shrunken head, a power source for the demon Vrachtung, which was adorned with a necklace of human toes. Vrachtung was one of the mayor's oldest acquaintances, and a heck of a card player.

The mayor took a moment to look closely at the string of toes and decided that his eyes were not playing tricks on him. The fourth toe from the right end, a toe that hung just below Vrachtung's tiny Adam's apple, had withered and blackened some time in the last few days.

Who was that?

The mayor searched his mind and finally found the memory he was seeking.

"Polly Snyder," he said softly to himself.

Such a nice lady. And a promising demon. I wonder what happened to her.

The mayor considered contacting Vrachtung to find out, but decided it could keep until the next biannual conclave. The withered toe told him that poor Polly was no longer living, dead, or undead. In time, that toe would fall from Vrachtung's necklace and disappear completely.

Poor dear, the Mayor thought. *I wonder if Cecil knows?*

Though Cecil Snyder had first placed himself in the mayor's power years earlier with this initial transaction, he had proved over the years to be a faithful lackey. The mayor no longer worried that his only hold over Snyder had been the knowledge of that old contract. Once he'd pulled the strings necessary to get him appointed as principal of Sunnydale High, he knew that Snyder would always be his to command.

The mayor made a quick mental note to send a brief condolence card to Cecil, then closed his secret cabinet and returned to his desk.

He had a very busy year ahead of him.

ABOUT THE AUTHOR

In addition to *One Thing or Your Mother*, **Kirsten Beyer** is the author of *Star Trek Voyager, String Theory: Fusion*; the Alias APO novel *Once Lost*; and contributed the short story "Isabo's Shirt" for the *Distant Shores Anthology*.

Last year Kirsten appeared in the Los Angeles productions of *Johnson over Jordan*, *This Old Planet*, and Harold Pinter's *The Hothouse*, which the *L.A. Times* called "unmissable." She also appeared in the Geffen Playhouse's world premiere of *Quills* and has been seen on *General Hospital* and *Passions*, among many others.

Kirsten has undergraduate degrees in English literature and theater arts, and a Masters of fine arts from UCLA. She is currently working on the feature film, *Directing for Dummies*, and a number of other original screenplays.

She lives in Los Angeles with her husband, David, and their very fat cat, Owen.